6/13

The Cheshire Cat's Eye

Other books by Marcia Muller:
Edwin of the Iron Shoes
Ask the Cards a Question

The Cheshire Cat's Eye

A Sharon McCone
Mystery by

MARCIA MULLER

ST. MARTIN'S PRESS · NEW YORK

Library of Congress Cataloging in Publication Data

Muller, Marcia.
  The Cheshire cat's eye.

  I. Title.
PS3563.U397C45 1983   813'.54   82–16919
ISBN 0-312-13175-5

10 9 8 7 6 5 4 3 2

For Bill Pronzini and one other individual,
who shall remain Nameless

The Cheshire Cat's Eye

1

The row of Victorian houses loomed dark in the early June fog. I put my hand on the cold iron railing and started up the stairway from the street. As I pushed through the overgrown front yard, blackberry vines reached out to tear at my clothing.

Strange, I thought, that there were no lights. The houses were under renovation, but surely Jake would have brought a flashlight to the one where he had asked me to meet him.

I went up the marble porch steps and felt for a doorbell. Nothing. Finally I got out my pencil flash and shone its beam around the leaded-glass doors. The bell hung on wires, broken. I started to knock, and the door swung inward.

I paused in the high-ceilinged vestibule. There was no sound. Maybe my friend had gotten tired of waiting; I was later than I'd said I would be. I decided to see if he'd left me a note.

I went through an arch and crossed the parlor toward the back of the house. Behind it was another room with an ornate fireplace, and beyond that another archway and blackness. I stepped through the archway and waited for my eyes to become accustomed to the dark. When they were, I inched toward a faintly outlined door at the rear. My foot hit something soft.

The back of my neck prickled. I turned on the flash again. It went out. I punched the faulty switch harder and shone the beam down, at the floor. At a man's prone body.

I recoiled, my heart pounding.

"Jake," I whispered. "Oh, no. Jake!"

Even at a glance, even in this light, I could tell my friend was dead. He lay on his side in what common sense told me must be blood. Only it didn't smell like blood.

My fingers clutched the flash. I stood for a moment, several moments. It seemed like hours. Finally I knelt and dipped my finger into the pool of liquid. It was thick and sticky. Paint. Bright-red house paint.

I straightened, wiping my finger on my jeans before I realized what I was doing.

"Oh, Jake," I said, louder. My words echoed in the cavernous room, and then the old house enveloped me in ponderous silence. From outside came the bellow of foghorns on San Francisco Bay.

I backed toward the wall, my eyes still on the body, and fumbled with a light switch. Nothing happened. When I cast my flash at the high ceiling it illuminated an ornate plaster rosette, but no fixture. The big Victorian had obviously been stripped.

Still, I didn't need a second look to make sure who the paint-smeared victim was. Jake Kaufmann, the friend who had so urgently requested I meet him here—my flashlight showed enough of his tanned face and black hair to identify him. Any closer investigation I'd leave for the police.

I backtracked to the hallway, glad to escape the presence of the corpse. Why, I thought, would anyone want to kill a gentle man like Jake Kaufmann? And why had he insisted we meet in this deserted house?

Stepping onto the porch, I spotted a phone booth on the far corner below. I ran down the steps and through the maze of wild vegetation to the stairway that scaled the retaining wall between there and the street. By the time I reached the booth my heart was pounding again.

Reflexively I checked my watch. It was 9:00 P.M. I dialed the SFPD and asked for Greg Marcus, head of Homicide. The lieutenant was off duty. Did I want to leave a message? No, I'd call him at home. I fished in my bag for my address book and redialed. He answered on the first ring.

"Greg," I said, "it's Sharon McCone."

"Hey, how's my favorite private eye?"

"Not so good, Greg. I've found a friend of mine murdered."

There was a pause. "Aren't you a little corpse-happy

lately?'' He was referring to two murder cases that I'd recently been involved with in his jurisdiction.

"Greg, I'm not kidding.''

"I didn't think you were.'' His tone became crisp. "Where are you?''

I gave him the address of the Victorian on Steiner Street.

"Stay put. A squad car will be along, and I'll get there as soon as I can.''

I hung up and stared at the phone for a moment before I got out another dime. Even when you're dating the head of Homicide, I told myself, it's wise to have your attorney there when you've found a body. And since my lawyer was also my boss at All Souls Legal Cooperative, I knew he'd want to be present. I dialed and asked Hank Zahn to come at once.

Outside the booth, I looked up at the house, whose turret and gables were shrouded in the fog. Its neighbors on the hill were similarly dark. The street was deserted, save for a lone black man who gave me a hostile glance as he passed. Pulling my jacket closer, I started toward the row of Victorians as a siren began to wail. The man quickly stepped into the shadows.

Two uniformed men sprang from the squad car when it pulled up. "You the one reported the body?''

"Yes.''

"Where is it?''

"Inside, third room from the front.'' I gestured up at the house.

One of the men climbed the stairway in the retaining wall. The other remained, his eyes on me. "Your identification, please.''

I produced my California private investigator's license. The officer's eyebrows raised as he examined it. "Private op, huh?''

I didn't answer.

"How'd you happen to be here?''

I sat down on the cold cement steps. "I'll talk to Lieutenant Marcus when he gets here.''

"You'd better talk now.''

I shook my head and leaned back, my elbows on the step behind me. Apparently the cop thought better of pressuring me, because he withdrew to the squad car.

I tried to focus on my observations and movements since I'd first arrived at the house, but the picture of Jake lying paint-smeared and dead kept flashing before me as the lab crew and inspectors arrived. I was unsuccessfully fighting off the image when a blue BMW pulled up and Greg Marcus hurried up the sidewalk.

He was a big blond-haired man wearing Levi's and a suede jacket. His bushy eyebrows, several shades darker than his hair, were drawn together in a frown. I stood, and he reached out a hand to steady me.

"You all right?"

"Of course I'm all right!" His concern served to sharpen my professional rivalry, already finely honed by our past encounters.

"Well, that's good," he snapped back. "I wouldn't want to see you with your composure rattled. What have you got on your face?"

"My face?"

"Yeah." He traced a line on my forehead with his thumb. "It's red."

"Oh." I felt the sticky encrustation. "It's probably paint. I must have rubbed it there without noticing. The body's in a pool of house paint."

"And you managed to get into it, too. Where is it?"

The uniformed officer came down the stairway. "Dining room, Lieutenant. Back of the first floor. The electricity's off, but the lab boys are setting up some lights."

Greg nodded and turned to me. "Stay here."

"Yes, *sir*."

"That's the spirit." He grinned and disappeared up the stairs.

I turned to see a taxi pull up to the curb. A lanky figure emerged. Hank Zahn, my boss. He paid the driver and came toward me, tugging at his trenchcoat, which enveloped his body like a scarecrow's clothes.

"What happened?" Hank's eyes, behind his thick horn-rimmed glasses, were anxious.

"Like I said on the phone, I found someone dead."

"Who?"

Before I could answer, Greg returned, putting a hand on my shoulder. "Okay, the lab boys have rigged up some portable lights in there. You come up with me, and we'll go over what happened." He added, to Hank, "What are you doing here?" He and Hank were old friends.

Hank scratched furiously at his Brillo pad of light-brown hair and glanced at me.

"I asked him to come," I said.

"Why? You didn't kill the victim, did you?"

"Of course not! But he is—was—one of our clients."

Hank's eyes widened behind his thick glasses. "Who?"

"Do you remember Jake Kaufmann?"

"Of course. The guy who paints the Victorians. He's been a client for years."

"Right. He called me earlier—"

"Wait a minute," Greg interrupted. "Start from the beginning. The victim's name is Kaufmann?"

I nodded. "Jake Kaufmann." Around us, the scene had exploded into a whirl of people and activity. A crowd had materialized, drawn by the lights and sirens. "Jake's what they call a color consultant. He specializes in painting Victorians that have been restored. He uses bright colors and intricate patterns. They're flamboyant. A lot of people detest them. Not, I don't think, enough to drown him in a pool of his own paint, if that's what happened." I realized I was rambling and reined myself in. "Anyway, he called me this afternoon and asked that I meet him here."

"Why?" Greg asked.

"I'm not sure. All he said was that he had found out something that frightened him and wanted me as a witness."

"Why you?"

"We were friends. I'd done some investigation for him before. A strange business that was, too."

Hank nodded emphatically.

"Anyway," I went on, "he thought he could trust me."

"And?"

"And I told him I had an evening conference at All Souls, so I couldn't make it at seven-thirty, when he asked. I said I'd be here as soon as I could. Only . . ." I paused, sick. My lateness might have precipitated Jake's murder.

"Okay," Greg said, glancing at a patrolman who was coming down the stairs in the retaining wall, "they're set up in there, so let's go over exactly what happened when you arrived. You," he added to Hank, "can wait here."

Relief showed plainly on Hank's face.

Greg steered me up the stairway. "Sure you'll be okay, hotshot?" His mouth quirked up sardonically, but his eyes were kind.

I squeezed his arm. "I'll be fine."

"Good." He nodded approvingly.

We continued up the walk to the columned entry, brushing aside runaway vegetation that reached out to touch us. From inside came a murmur of voices.

Greg said, "You came in here, through the front door?"

"Yes." I ignored my apprehension about seeing Jake's body again and concentrated on relating the facts. We crossed the hallway to the arch and entered the parlor. In the light that now streamed from the rear of the house, I saw another tiled fireplace with a high mantel. "I went through here, to the back parlor, and then to the dining room." Greg followed me. Our footsteps clattered on the bare floors.

At the archway to the dining room, I stopped, sucking in my breath. The harsh glare of the portable floodlights made the red paint a thousand times more garish, Jake's pallor even more ghastly. A ladder, which the beam of my flashlight hadn't picked up earlier, stood near the body, and an overturned paint can and brush lay on the floor.

"Maybe it was an accident," I said in a small voice.

"No way." Greg stepped around me. "I'll show you."

Reluctantly, I followed him. Jake lay with one arm out-stretched, the other crumpled under him. His khaki work clothes were splattered with red.

"See this?" Greg indicated a discolored indentation behind Jake's left ear. "There's no possibility that could have been caused by a fall from a ladder, given the way he's lying. I guess it was made with the proverbial blunt instrument. And, if you look around, you'll see other things that are inconsistent with an accident theory."

I looked. "Such as the fact that he would have been painting in the dark."

"Right."

"And that he would have been painting a wall that was unprepared." I indicated several deep cracks in the plaster. "And," I added, "that he was using exterior paint on an interior wall."

"You've got it."

"Good Lord." I stared down at the dead man. "Then some-body tried to fake an accident."

"Somebody who doesn't know much about the painting trade."

"But why?"

Greg shrugged and went to talk with one of the lab techni-cians.

I continued to stare down. The floor was littered with chunks of plaster, strips of wallpaper, and sawdust. The wainscot-ing and leaded-glass cabinets had been prepared for refinishing. In the rubble at my feet were bits of multicolored glass and an ornate tubular metal fitting, the socket of a broken light bulb protruding from it. Troubled, I glanced up at the rosette on the ceiling. There was no evidence of a light fixture having hung there.

Greg returned to me. "Show me where you touched the paint."

I pointed to a spot where the surface was disturbed.

"Touch anything else?"

"The wall, and the light switch."

He nodded briskly. "That's all I need from you now, but I want a statement tonight. There's a place around the corner called Johnny's Kansas City Barbecue that's reasonably clean and safe, for this neighborhood. Wait for me there, and I'll drive you to the Hall."

"Okay. Hank will keep me company."

Greg turned back to the technicians, kicking aside the small metal fitting on the floor as he did so. Obviously it wasn't a clue—to him. I reached down and pocketed it.

2

The sign in the window of Johnny's Kansas City Barbecue said OPEN, but there were no customers at the oilcloth-covered tables. When Hank and I entered, a big black man with grizzled hair emerged from a swinging door at the rear, wiping his hands on his stained chef's apron.

"We're not serving anymore," he said, "but the bar's still open."

Hank looked questioningly at me. I nodded. A drink sounded like a good idea. We climbed onto high-backed stools, and the man placed cocktail napkins in front of us.

"What'll it be?"

Hank ordered scotch on the rocks, and I ordered bourbon. Our host poured and withdrew to what presumably was the kitchen.

Hank raised his glass. "Here's to the memory of a pretty nice guy."

I returned the toast and sipped, melancholy washing

through me with the liquor. "Jake *was* nice, dammit."

"He was a real craftsman, the kind you don't find much anymore. I remember once he suggested he do a color plan for All Souls. He said houses should be cheerful, human habitations, not dingy prisons of wood and stone."

While I wouldn't go so far as to call it a prison, the big brown Victorian that housed All Souls was drab. "So why didn't you do it?"

Hank shrugged. "It wasn't in the budget."

Nothing extra ever was. A legal-services plan that charged its members on a sliding fee scale seldom had large cash reserves.

I was silent for a moment.

Hank asked, "You dated Jake for a while, didn't you?"

"Yes. It was when I was breaking off with my musician friend down south. Jake was gentle, understanding . . ." My voice choked up and, to cover it, I sipped my drink.

"He's married now, isn't he?"

I nodded. "Six months ago, to a divorcee named Judy Riggs. She has two kids. Jake always liked kids. They made a nice family. I wonder who gets to tell her."

"You're not close to his wife?"

"I hardly know her. I haven't seen Jake himself since they married."

"You say Greg is meeting us here?"

"Right."

"Then it'll probably be me. He'll come in and say, 'Listen, Hank, since Jake was an All Souls client, would you mind . . .'"

I smiled faintly. Hank did a creditable imitation of the lieutenant. When I looked at him, though, there was real pain in his eyes. My boss genuinely cared for all his clients, and too often made their troubles his. Breaking the news to Jake's family would be no small ordeal, but Hank would prefer to suffer it than to have them told impersonally by a cop.

"You know what bothers me?" I asked.

"What?"

"The crime is so meaningless. Who would want to kill Jake?"

"Maybe he was killed by a burglar."

"What's there to steal?"

"True. A vandal, then. There's a lot of vandalism in this neighborhood."

"A vandal wouldn't have gone to the trouble of faking an accident."

"An accident?"

Briefly I explained about the paint and the ladder at the scene. "So you see," I finished, "someone killed him deliberately and then tried to cover up. That's borne out by the fact he said he was frightened when he called me."

The proprietor stuck his grizzled head out of the kitchen, and Hank signaled for another round. We watched him pour the drinks with a practiced flourish. Setting them down, he said, "You folks ain't been in before."

"First time," I replied.

"Thought so. I got a good memory for faces. 'Course I don't get too many white faces here."

I looked at him to see if it might be a warning, but his dusky features were bland. He leaned against the back bar, arms folded across his aproned chest.

"You the owner?" I asked.

"Yeah. Johnny Hart's the name."

"I'm Sharon McCone, and this is Hank Zahn. Have you been in this location a long time?"

"Ten years this coming October."

"Get mostly local customers?"

"Mostly."

"Tell me something: that block of empty Victorians on the hill above Steiner Street, are they being restored?"

"That's what I hear."

"Who owns the big house on the corner? The one with the tower."

"Same people as own all the others. Wintringham and Associates, they're called."

"What do they do, buy up old wrecks and restore them?"

"Yeah. They'll spiff them up and make a killing selling them to middle-class whites." He grinned mockingly.

"How is it they managed to get hold of an entire block?"

"Wintringham—David, his first name is—inherited it. His father was an architect who made a pile building houses after the Second World War. Stucco houses out in the Avenues. Modern, for then. But he always lived right here, in that big one on the corner, and he kept buying up and down the street. When he died, the son got it all."

"Was the big house what you'd call the family mansion?"

"Guess so. Why else would he have stayed? He could have lived anyplace."

I sipped my drink. "Can they get much for the houses, even fixed up, in this neighborhood?"

"Sure can. You should see what's buying in here: fairies like Wintringham, young families, rich white lawyers." Hart's voice dripped scorn.

Beside me, Hank stiffened.

"What's wrong with him?" Johnny Hart demanded.

"He's a white lawyer, but not rich."

"Too bad for him. Hey, man, it's nothing personal. That's just what's moving in. I don't care who buys those places, so long as my business picks up."

"But some people care," I said.

"Sure, folks that've been here all their lives, living cheap in rundown buildings. The places sell, they're kicked out, can't find anything they can afford. All of a sudden they're on the outs in the neighborhood where they came up. You can see how they feel." He smiled wickedly, leaning across the bar and showing yellowed teeth. "Or maybe you can't. Maybe, to you, they're just niggers."

I blinked. After a pause, Hank cleared his throat.

Johnny Hart laughed. "Hey, don't look that way! It's just

a word; can't hurt no one. And you," he added to me, "ought to know that. From that thick black hair and those high cheekbones, I'd say you got a touch of Indian blood."

"Shoshone," I said.

"And it's probably caused you some grief in your time. So don't go getting that uptight liberal look. That's for him to do." He pointed to Hank, who gulped his drink and began to cough.

I was starting to like our host. "Somehow, I've never felt much like an Indian," I said. "I'm only an eighth, and no one else in my family resembles one in the slightest."

"What's the other seven-eighths?"

"Scotch-Irish."

"Huh. So what brings you to these parts tonight?"

Before I could answer, the door opened and a young black man in a leather coat and cowboy hat came in. "Hey, Johnny," he said.

"How's it going, Ray?"

The young man glanced suspiciously at Hank and me. "Some to-do around the corner. Dude got himself killed in one of those empty houses."

Hart's eyes flicked to me and then back to the newcomer. "Anybody we know?"

"Nah, just some white dude who paints houses for Wintringham."

"Which house was he in?"

"Big one with the tower, on the corner."

"You don't say." Hart turned to me, his face stony. "Seems like you've been playing a little game, lady," he said softly.

"I . . ."

"What's it to you, who owns those places? And why all the questions?" He leaned across the bar, eyes narrowed.

I bit my lip and shifted uncomfortably on the barstool.

"Well?" Hart prompted.

Just then the door opened again, and Greg strode in. "There you are," he said. "Let's go."

I jumped to my feet and grabbed my bag. Johnny Hart

glared menacingly. I looked away from him.

To Hank, Greg said, "By the way, Hank, since you were the victim's attorney, could you . . . ?"

Hank held up a hand. "I'm way ahead of you."

3

"You certainly killed two birds with one stone," I said to Greg as we entered the Homicide squad room.

He turned innocent blue eyes to me. "I don't know what you mean."

"You got rid of an unpleasant task and you got rid of my attorney."

"You don't need an attorney if you have nothing to hide."

"Yeah." I assumed a tough-guy voice. "That's what they all say right before they throw you in the slammer."

He opened the door to his cubicle and glared down at me as I ducked under his outstretched arm. "What is it with you private operatives? You all sound like you've read too many paperback detective novels."

"Well, of course."

With an interested glance, Greg waved me toward a chair. "Really? You read stuff like that?"

"When I was at Berkeley, I worked nights as a security guard to make my tuition. When you sit hour after hour, watching over an empty building that no one in his right mind would want to break into, you'll read anything."

He shook his head in disbelief and punched the intercom to summon a steno, then leaned back in his chair, hands clasped at the nape of his neck. His gaze was steady and neutral. I returned it.

"You do turn up in the right places at the right times," Greg finally said.

"Or the wrong places, depending on how you look at it."

He nodded. "We still on for dinner tomorrow?"

"If I'm not in jail."

"You won't be. You're too smart not to cooperate." Abruptly, he swiveled to look out the window, which faced a blank wall. I wondered what he saw there, or what he avoided seeing over here.

In my short acquaintance with Greg Marcus, I gradually had been forced to abandon my initial stereotype of him as the hard-bitten homicide cop. True, he had a toughness that expressed itself in disciplined movements and deliberate speech. But he was also a gentle man, who loved art and classical music and puttering in his Twin Peaks garden. He had a capacity for fury that matched my own, but he was saved from it by a heightened sense of the absurd. I had begun to like the lieutenant, like him a lot. And not the least of my liking stemmed from the fact that, at forty-one, he had a lean body, a smile that crinkled the lines around his eyes, and thick blond hair I had had occasion to run my hands through.

But he still managed to piss me off on the average of once a week.

The steno entered, and Greg swiveled around, lit a cigarette, and began a formal interview that covered roughly the same ground as we had at the crime scene. "Now," he finally said, "we'll go into the background. You say you'd previously done some investigation for the deceased."

"Yes. It would have been . . ." I paused. "A year ago last July."

"Describe it, please."

"As I mentioned before," I began, "Jake was a color consultant. But before that, he was an ordinary house-painter. He contracted out to big developments, like the tracts that were built in the Avenues in the fifties and in Daly City in the sixties." I stopped. Was it possible Jake had worked for David Wintringham's father? Did that, in some dim way, explain why he had met his death in the Wintringhams' old house?

Greg's eyes narrowed. "What is it?"

I shook my head. "Nothing." Greg had accused me before of relying too much on coincidence—or "woman's intuition," as he tauntingly called it. "I'm having difficulty remembering dates," I hedged. "Have you heard of something called the Colorist Movement?"

"No."

"It started in the sixties, slowly at first, then picked up speed in the days of the so-called flower children. Essentially, what happened was that people started sprucing up Victorians that had been neglected. Only they didn't paint them in neutrals, or even in one color. There's a place on Steiner Street, not far from the crime scene, that pretty well explains what the movement is about. They call it the 'psychedelic house,' and, believe me, it is. They painted on as many colors as they could, using tiny artists' brushes and—"

"I know the one you mean, but what's that got to do with Kaufmann's murder? Most of the Victorians that have been rehabilitated have multicolored paint jobs."

"Yes, but they didn't back then. And neighbors were outraged by the explosions of color. They associated it with hippies, drugs. Finally, the new style gained acceptance, but only over strong opposition."

"And Jake Kaufmann?" Greg insisted.

"He was one of the first to experiment with color, on his own house, and then on others. His method was to consult with the owners and draw up a detailed scheme for each individual house. Soon his services were in such demand that he had a two-year waiting list."

"And now where do you fit in?"

I knew Greg was irritated with my rambling account, so I tried to pare it down. "There's this woman, Eleanor van Dyne. She's one of those matron-crusader types, heads an organization called Salvation Incorporated. It's dedicated to preserving historical buildings."

"Like the Foundation for San Francisco's Architectural Heritage?"

"Yes, and the Preservation Group, and the Victorian Alliance."

"Jesus, and the Committee to Save the Fake Rocks. Can you

believe that one?" Greg was referring to a cliff on the Great Highway that was constructed entirely of wire and stucco. San Franciscans would try to save anything.

"Go on," Greg said, glancing at the steno and appearing embarrassed at his unprofessional digression. It would not do for my statement to sound like a casual conversation.

"This van Dyne person is very traditional. She believes buildings should be restored to their exact original state. And bright color was something the Victorians didn't go in for; most of their houses were pretty dour. Needless to say, Eleanor van Dyne took off after Jake. When he painted a house on her street in Pacific Heights three shades of purple with pink and gold trim, she filed suit against him for creating an eyesore."

"I guess! And you gathered evidence for his defense?"

"Yes. I interviewed the neighbors about how they felt, talked to the owners of the house, researched the Colorist Movement."

"What was the outcome?"

"Van Dyne dropped the suit. She really didn't have much of a case but, more than that, I think she was influenced by her personal feelings for Jake. In spite of their differing philosophies, she was fond of him. She considered him a real craftsman who had gone astray, and she hoped she could bring him around to her way of thinking."

"Did she?"

"Not that I know of."

"Did you have any further contact with the deceased between the time the suit was dropped and when he called you today?"

I hesitated. "We dated a few times, close to a year ago."

"Oh?" There was an interested note in his voice.

Inwardly I smiled. "Yes. It was no great romance. He got married soon after that."

"I see." Greg nodded, his face a blank. "And this phone call—he didn't identify who he was meeting?"

"No." There was something, but. . . . Tired, I pressed my fingertips to my temples.

Greg was silent for a moment, then dismissed the steno. He sat slumped in his chair, regarding me thoughtfully. "I want to ask one more question, strictly between you and me."

"Yes?"

"Are you holding anything back?"

I widened my eyes. "Why would I?"

"You didn't answer the question."

"I've given you as complete a statement as I can at this time."

He continued to stare at me. "A simple yes or no never suffices for you, does it?"

"Guess not."

Abruptly he stood. "Okay, that's it. I'll have one of my men drive you back to your car."

I got up and started for the door.

"Oh, papoose," he added, using his private nickname for me, which I loathed.

"Yes, sir?" I replied acidly.

"Don't forget about dinner tomorrow."

4

I resisted the ring of the telephone, pulling over my head quilts that were twisted from a night of bad dreams involving paint-smeared corpses. The ringing went on. Finally I stuck out an arm, knocking something heavy off the nightstand, and grabbed the receiver.

"Huh?"

"Sharon?" It was Katy, daytime operator at my answering service. "I know you don't like to be bothered on Saturday mornings, but the guy said it was about a murder, and I thought . . ."

"Wait a minute." I struggled to a sitting position and looked to see what I had knocked on the floor. It was a book: Silberman's five-hundred-forty-page *Criminal Violence, Criminal Justice.* I'd been keeping my hand in my old field, sociology.

"Okay," I said into the receiver, "what's going on?"

"A David Wintringham is on the line. He needs to talk to you about a . . . no, *the* murder. Should I—?"

"I'll talk to him."

The voice that came on was nasal. "Ms. McCone?"

"Yes."

"You're the Ms. McCone who discovered Jake Kaufmann's body last night? The private detective?"

"Yes, I am. How did—?"

"Never mind. There isn't time. I'm the owner of the house where you found him, and I would like very much to talk with you."

"All right. Talk."

"In person, I mean. Could you come over here this morning?"

It was Saturday. I'd planned to clean the apartment. I'd planned to grocery shop. I'd much rather talk about Jake's murder, though. "I could manage that."

"Good. Before noon?"

"I'll do what I can. Where are you located?"

"At the Victorian block on Steiner Street. Go to the Italianate house at the opposite end from the . . . the death house and ask for me there. If I'm on a job site, they'll direct you."

"Go to the what?"

"Oh, of course, you can't be expected to know the styles. It's the house at the far end of the block, the only one that's been painted. We have our offices and residence there. I'll expect you."

"Right."

"And, Ms. McCone . . . thank you."

I replaced the receiver and momentarily contemplated the sunlight falling across the bed. It was still early. There was plenty of time before I had to get up. I lay back under the quilts and huddled there in a pensive mood, remembering the first time I'd met Jake Kaufmann.

I'd hunted him down at a job site in the Haight, perched high on a scaffold, surrounded by paints. When I shouted who I was, he shouted that he didn't have time to come down, but if I wanted I could come up. So up I went and sat, my legs dangling in the air while Jake painted. After five years with All Souls, I was used to interviewing our often-eccentric clients anywhere.

Of Eleanor van Dyne's suit, Jake could only say, "How can she do such a thing? Does that woman not know beauty? Does she not understand? Look at the cherub up there on that frieze." He pointed, his diminutive frame leaning back at such a sharp angle that I had to close my eyes. When I looked up, I saw the carving, a blissful smile on its face, wings spread.

"Do you know what I'm going to do with that?" Jake demanded. "The smile, such a smile should be highlighted in red. And the wings—a rainbow of wings. That cherub is a treasure, a gift from God—as well as the architect of this house, bless him—and I'm going to bring forth its glory."

As he spoke, I reflected that I could understand van Dyne's point. But to Jake, a riot of color was beauty. All the time he described his cherub, he gyrated on the balls of his feet, black eyes flashing in his tanned face. "A treasure, a gift, that's what it is. My color will pull it out of the grime and obscurity so everyone can enjoy it. Tell me, does that woman have no sense of what I'm doing? Does she not feel?" He spread his arms, about to fly like the cherub above. "No," he said sadly, lowering them. "No, I fear not. That woman will never understand."

Jake had been a passionate craftsman. I would not meet many more like him. It angered me that someone had snuffed out his life, and I wanted that someone found.

To that end, I thought back to our conversation of late yesterday afternoon.

"I'm frightened," he had said. "Probably I shouldn't be, but at any rate, I need a witness."

"Frightened of what?" I asked.

"Something I've found out."

"And what do you want me to witness?"

There was a pause. "I don't want to talk about it over the phone. Suffice it to say that the person I'm meeting is unreliable . . . gets tanked up. Will you be there?"

"But, Jake, can't you tell me—"

"Please, Sharon." The strain was evident in his voice. "Just meet me."

And I'd said I would.

And now Jake was dead.

My fault? Not really. But then again, I owed something to Jake, to find his killer, this killer who got "tanked up," who drank too much. Unfortunately, San Francisco was not a town known for sobriety. Still . . .

I threw off the quilts, started coffee, and hopped into the shower. The needle spray on my upturned face revived me and lifted my spirits. If I could drum up a job via my interview with David Wintringham, maybe I could finance my own search for Jake's killer—and what a chance that would be to show up Lieutenant Gregory Marcus.

I arrived at Steiner Street forty-five minutes later, dressed in jeans and a sweater, my hair blowing loose in the mild June breeze. The house Wintringham had directed me to was a yellow-and-blue structure with angled bay windows and a columned porch, very similar to the building that housed All Souls. I went up to the door and complied with the sign that ordered me to enter.

A stocky, pug-faced man wearing designer jeans and a green velvet jacket stood behind a desk in the hallway. He looked up, little eyes appraising me from head to toe, then wandering over my shoulder, as if he expected to see someone more interesting there.

"Yeah?" His tone was distant.

"Sharon McCone, to see Mr. Wintringham."

The man's face underwent a sudden transformation to a mocking grin. "Oh, yeah, the rent-a-cop. Wonder what half-assed idea he'll come up with next?"

It was not a greeting I had anticipated. "Don't know," I responded mildly. "Is he here?"

"He's on a job site, said for you to meet him there." He paused, fingering a heavy gold chain that hung against the expanse of chest exposed by his unbuttoned shirt. "You think you can do it, McCone?"

"Do what?"

"Solve all of David's problems?"

"Does he have problems?"

"You ought to know. You found it."

"It?" I couldn't keep the irritation out of my voice.

"The mortal remains of Jake Kaufmann."

"Look, Mr. . . ."

"French. Larry French. I'm Wintringham's business partner."

The name was vaguely familiar. "Look, Mr. French, I'd better discuss this with your partner. You say he's on a job site?"

"Yeah, two doors down at the little Stick-style place."

"Stick?"

"Yeah. It's a kind of Victorian architecture, but I guess *you* wouldn't know that."

I was getting tired of having people presume my ignorance, however vast. I shrugged off my irritation with French, though, and started for the door.

"Hey, McCone?"

I whirled on him. "Yes?"

"Sure you can find it?"

I didn't favor him with a reply as I went out. To reach the other house, I would either have to cut a path through the pyracantha and pine and blackberry vines that choked the front yards or descend to the street and climb back up again by that house's stairway. I chose the latter.

The "Stick-style" house was smaller and had more severe lines than the one I had just left. The facade had been covered with beige stucco, and there were boards missing on the front steps. From inside came angry voices. I climbed to the porch and listened.

" . . . a perfectly decent craftsman until you hired him and dragged him down to your level." The speaker was female, and shrill.

"I had nothing to do with the change in the direction of Jake's work. That happened long before I came on the scene." I recognized David Wintringham by his nasal tones.

"You may not have caused it, but you certainly encouraged it."

A second female voice murmured something.

"And don't you talk!" the first woman cried. "Look at you—the product of the finest design schools, producing these abominations so your sleazy boyfriend can make a fast buck. You should be ashamed, Charmaine! Completely and utterly ashamed!"

Charmaine, whoever she was, murmured again.

"Don't you speak to me like that, you cheap little slut! I know there's nothing you wouldn't stoop to for him! Better you stick to dabbling with your stained glass than this!"

The other woman began to cry.

"Leave her alone!" Wintringham's voice trembled with anger.

"You would defend her! You dragged her into this, just like you did poor Jake. David, they may speak badly of your father's work, but at least he was honest."

"Honest! You're a fine one to talk about my father's honesty."

"We won't go into that. But mark my words, David. The preservationist world isn't going to forget what you did to Jake Kaufmann. You encouraged him in his atrocities, exploited him, and now look what's happened. Frankly, I wouldn't be a bit surprised if you'd killed him!"

High-heeled shoes strode imperiously across the floor, and the door in front of me swung open. A tall woman with immaculately coiffed gray-blond hair confronted me: Eleanor van Dyne, in a fashionable linen suit, her fingers bedecked with rings. As on both of the occasions when I'd seen her two years before, I was struck by her legs, which were surprisingly good for a woman in her late fifties.

In spite of coming face-to-face with me, van Dyne's eyes were devoid of recognition. She sniffed angrily and swept down the steps, a hurricane of indignation. I watched her careen off in a white Mercedes.

From within the house came the sound of the other woman's crying and Wintringham's soothing remarks. I waited a minute and then knocked.

"Enter!" Wintringham growled.

They were in the parlor, in front of a ceramic-tiled fireplace that appeared to have been walled up and partially uncovered. Charmaine, a tiny Japanese woman, was dabbing at her eyes with a tissue. She wore a pale suede jumpsuit and, when she turned to look at me, her hair swung out in a soft bell. David Wintringham, a gaunt, hawk-nosed man, presented a marked contrast to Charmaine's chic in his paint-stained work clothes. His dark hair was unruly, and he pushed it back from his forehead in an impatient gesture. They both looked as if I'd caught them with their hands in the cookie jar.

I introduced myself, and Wintringham came forward. Charmaine flung her tissue toward the fireplace and, kneeling, began to fiddle with some wallpaper and fabric samples that were spread on the floor. She quickly gave it up as a useless effort and rocked back on her heels, regarding Wintringham and me. Her hands, which had red talon-like nails, clenched and unclenched spasmodically.

"I'm sorry I couldn't meet you at the office," Wintringham said smoothly. "A construction zone isn't the most desirable place to talk, but Charmaine and I had to go over the decoration scheme she plans for the house."

I glanced around dubiously. The sheetrock, where it had been ripped off the fireplace, was jagged, and the tape between the other sections was clearly visible. The floor was covered with worn gold carpeting. I had the sense of a construction project halted midway and briefly wondered if Wintringham's restoration were in financial trouble.

Wintringham caught my expression. "Yes, this house has been butchered. In the fifties it was made over into modern apartments: They walled up all the fireplaces, removed most of the original fixtures, threw up cheap paneling, carpeted over the hardwood."

"Why would someone want to do that?"

"Modern apartments were in big demand back then. It's hard to imagine, but my friend Paul lived here for a while, and the place looked like something out of *Architectural Digest,* all bright colors and Danish furniture."

I myself preferred modern things, but it still seemed senseless to ruin a classic old house that way. "It looks like you have a lot of work cut out for you before it will be restored to the original state. Isn't it premature to think about decor?"

"Not really. We settle on that at the very start of the work. That way, if structural changes are required, like adding pillars or reconstructing a fireplace, we can plan for them. By the way, this is my interior designer, Charmaine."

The tiny woman smiled. "Just Charmaine."

"I'm sorry?"

"It's the only name I go by."

"Oh. Well, it's a pretty name. Why spoil it?"

She bowed her head, bell-like hair swinging gracefully.

I turned to Wintringham. "Was that Eleanor van Dyne I saw leaving?"

He stiffened, but recovered quickly. "Yes. Do you know her?"

"Not well. I met her twice, back when she was suing Jake Kaufmann for putting too much color in her life."

Wintringham didn't see any humor in the remark. His face darkened, and a muscle twitched in his cheek. "That woman is such a bitch! She's always got to poke her nose in where it doesn't belong. If I can't find a way to stop her, she'll wreck this entire project."

"How?"

"Legal blocks. If there's such a thing as a legal groupie, that's what Eleanor is. Loves spending time in court."

"What sort of actions does she take?"

"Hauls you up before City Planning. Pulls out obscure ordinances to delay you. Tries to get injunctions and restraining orders. She's got this attorney—a litigious son-of-a-bitch. It's the perfect example of a crazy person finding a crazy lawyer, and whammo!" Wintringham slammed his fist into his palm.

"David, David," Charmaine interjected, "be calm."

"How can I be calm? Between that woman and Jake's murder and the vandals and the junkies scaring off prospective buyers, we're likely to go bust."

As I'd suspected, the project was in trouble.

"Mrs. van Dyne means well." Charmaine stood, dusting off her pale jumpsuit, even though she hadn't touched the floor. "She really is dedicated to preserving the Victorians. Without her, hundreds would have been razed. She just looks at it differently than you."

"I'll say she does! To Eleanor, anyone who makes a profit off them is a villain. Of course, she can afford to have that attitude, what with her financier husband and her mansion in Pacific Heights, and—"

Charmaine held up a red-taloned hand. "Enough. You didn't ask Miss McCone here to listen to a diatribe against Eleanor."

Wintringham's eyes swung to me, warily. "Charmaine's right, of course. Forgive me; the woman makes me so furious. Did you, by any chance, hear what she was saying to us?"

The question was casual, but calculated. I paused, recalling van Dyne's words: *Frankly, I wouldn't be a bit surprised if you'd killed him.*

"No," I said. "No. I was just coming up the stairs when she stormed out of here."

5

"I've been reminded of my ignorance about Victorian architecture a couple of times this morning," I said as Wintringham, Charmaine, and I descended the steep cement stairway in the wall. "Could you give me a quick rundown on the five houses in this block?"

Wintringham smiled broadly. It was clear that Victorians were his chief enthusiasm. "You picked a good block to study. It's unusual in that it represents each of the three major types of Victorian home: two Italianates, two Sticks, and a Queen Anne."

"Which is the Queen Anne?"

"The . . . er . . . ." He paused. "The house on the end, with the tower."

I sensed the reason for his hesitation: He didn't want to call it the "death house" again.

"They're by and large the most distinctive style left, and there are only around three hundred and fifty of them still standing in the city," he went on. "The tower, of course, is what most people associate with it. And the gables, the angled bay windows below them, the fish-scale shingling. There are, in fact, Queen Anne row houses without towers, but what you see here is the epitome of the style."

"When was that one built?"

"Eighteen-ninety. Usually they're more difficult to date, because most of the property records were burned in the fire after the earthquake of oh-six. This was our family mansion, so I happen to know." Wintringham gestured up at the house we'd just left. "Now that and the one next to it are San Francisco Sticks. Sometimes they're called Eastlakes, after the architect who pioneered the style. The word 'stick,' though, pretty much describes it: straight and severe. They have square bays, a flat roofline, and lots of free-style decorations like flowers or rosettes."

I glanced at Charmaine. She was watching me intently, as if anxious I should take all this in.

Wintringham started down the sidewalk with a brisk gait. "These two Sticks were built in eighteen-eighty-one or thereabouts. Compare them with the last two, which are Italianate."

I looked up at the houses: one, where I had met French, restored, the other not. "Their lines are softer," I said. "The bay windows have angled sides. The roofline is flat, though, like the Sticks."

"But it's corniced," Charmaine put in. "And the porches have Corinthian columns."

Wintringham beamed at her. I wondered if he were the boyfriend about whom Eleanor van Dyne had berated Charmaine. But hadn't Johnny Hart called him a "fairy"? He exhibited few of the stereotypical characteristics of homosexuals, but then it had been my experience that many didn't.

"The Italianates," Wintringham said as we started up the stairway in the wall below his headquarters, "were the earliest San Francisco Victorians. These two date from eighteen-eighty-eight or -nine. The reason I know, again, is that this one was the family home, before the Queen Anne was built."

We entered through the double doors off the columned porch. As before, Larry French stood behind the desk in the hall.

"Ahah, I see she found you," he announced with a leer. "Good work, McCone!"

I tried not to grit my teeth.

"Listen, David," French went on, "we better get out to Fort Mason. The show opens at noon."

"Paul's already there," Wintringham replied. "He can take care of the booth for a while."

"Paul?" French snorted, then added with elaborately feigned embarrassment, "Ooooops, David! I didn't mean to bad-mouth your sweetie!"

Wintringham didn't even look annoyed. Probably he was inured to French. "Did anyone ever tell you you're one hell of an unpleasant character, Larry?" he asked mildly.

Wintringham's comment also left French unruffled. "Sure. McCone here thinks so, but she's too polite to say. That right, McCone?"

"Now that you mention it."

Wintringham turned to me. "Don't let Larry get to you. His hobby is rubbing people the wrong way."

"Seriously, David," French went on, "I'm going over to the show. And you," he added to Charmaine, "had better haul your cute little butt over there with me."

Charmaine tossed her head, her dark hair hiding whatever expression was on her face.

"I said, get your ass in gear."

"I will drive myself, thank you." She walked stiffly down the hall toward the rear of the house.

"Women," French muttered. He picked up a set of car keys from the desk and exited, jingling them.

Wintringham heaved a sigh. "Let's go in the parlor." He led me to a room that was beautifully appointed with velvet sofas, marble-topped tables, and a crystal chandelier. "Again, let me apologize for my partner. I didn't pick him for his charm."

"What, then?"

"His money. What else?" Wintringham flung his gaunt frame onto a delicate chair, and I sat on the couch.

"This is a lovely room," I said, motioning at the mirrored fireplace and brocade draperies.

"Thank you. My friend Paul Collins and I live here as well as maintain offices, so we made it as homey as possible."

"Did Charmaine decorate it?"

"Yes. She's good, isn't she?"

"Very."

"Of course, Eleanor van Dyne doesn't think so. That's because she doesn't make everything authentic, down to the last detail." He stared off gloomily, his chin sunk onto his bony chest.

"Is the van Dyne problem why you wanted to see me?"

"Huh?" He jerked out of his reverie. "Oh, no, not at all. It's the murder. The police talked to me last night, but by then you'd already gone. Can you tell me about . . . about what you found? The police weren't very informative."

They weren't paid to be. I gave Wintringham as brief a version as possible.

When I had finished, he remained sprawled in the little chair, his expression thoughtful. Had I imagined a flicker of relief when I'd mentioned the faked accident? If so, it was gone now, replaced by moodiness.

I decided to seize the opportunity. "Mr. Wintringham—"

"David."

"David. Doesn't it strike you that it might be to your advantage to find Jake's killer?"

He looked up. "How so?"

"The crime did happen on your property, to one of your employees. I would think you'd feel some responsibility."

"Of course I'm concerned . . ."

"What if the murder had something to do with this project? Someone may wish to stop it. The murder may only be the beginning."

He frowned. "Won't the police find that out?"

I shrugged. "Maybe. Maybe not."

He jumped up and began pacing. "I don't know. I have little faith in the police myself, I admit."

"Often a private operative has more freedom to investigate than the officials."

"A private operative like you?"

"Exactly."

He stopped in front of me. "You want a job."

"I want to find Jake's killer, same as you."

"And be paid for it."

"It would take my time. I have to live."

"Doesn't All Souls pay you?"

"My time is billed to our clients, so . . ."

"I see."

He shuffled his feet indecisively. "I don't know. I don't have much money. It's all tied up in the project."

"Our rates are reasonable."

He nodded. "On the other hand, like I said, I don't have much faith in the police. Not after my last experience with them."

"What was that?"

He resumed pacing on the Oriental rug. "Three years ago there was another murder in that house."

"Who?"

He turned to me. The expression on his face was complex, tugging between sorrow and . . . what? I couldn't define it. "My father, Richard Wintringham. Perhaps you've heard of him."

"He was an architect," I said, recalling what Johnny Hart had told Hank and me.

"Yes." Wintringham sprawled in the chair again. "An architect, of sorts. He designed the Wintringham row houses. There are hundreds of them out in the Avenues."

"They're stucco, each attached to the other."

Wintringham's smile was taut with embarrassment. "You don't have to be polite, Sharon. They're dreary little boxes with two eyes of a window and a grinning mouth of a garage below. A critic once said that if you put a chain across the garage door, they would look like they were wearing braces. But after the war, they were a reasonable response to the housing shortage. And it's to my father's credit that he never went so far as to live in one."

"Your father lived in the Queen Anne?"

"And met his death there."

"Exactly how did he die?"

"The police theorized that he surprised a burglar. A number of valuable objects were taken, small things that could easily be carried away."

"Any of them ever turn up?"

"No."

"And I take it the killer was never caught."

"There were no clues."

"When did this happen?"

"Almost three years ago, on the twenty-sixth of May."

"What was the cause of death?"

"A blow to the head."

I looked up. My eyes met his. The way Jake had been killed.

"Are the police aware of the similarity?" I asked.

"Yes, but they didn't seem particularly interested."

"No, they wouldn't be. They'd just consider it a coincidence."

"Do you?"

"I'm not sure." I paused. I tend not to like coincidence as an explanation for similar events. "Perhaps the two are related. I might be able to find out something about your father's death by investigating Jake's." But even as I said it I felt it to be a cheap trick. Three-year-old murders are difficult, if not impossible, to solve.

Wintringham, however, looked thoughtful.

I pressed my advantage. "Will you hire me?"

He bit his lip. "I guess I have no choice. I want to get to the bottom of this—of both of the murders."

Again I felt a twinge of guilt, but only a twinge. Who knew what I'd turn up? "Good. Now, there's a minor problem. Technically I can only work for clients of All Souls." At his dismayed look, I held up my hand and went on. "But that's easily overcome. The way All Souls works, you pay a small yearly membership fee and you're charged on a sliding scale, according to your income. All you have to do is fill in our application and pay the fee, and we'll be in business."

He sat up briskly. "Do you have an application with you?"

I smiled. "Sure do."

While Wintringham filled it out, I wandered into the hall, studying the oil paintings that hung there. A door at the rear of the building opened, and Charmaine came out. She had repaired her smeared eye makeup and put on an overwhelming amount of heavy perfume.

"Do you have the time?" she asked in a harried voice.

"It's eleven-thirty."

"Ah, good. I'll make it."

"What is it you're going to, some kind of show?"

"There's a Victorian home exhibition at Fort Mason, Pier Three." She named a former army supply base that was now used for a variety of cultural activities. "Everyone who's anyone in the restoration field will have a booth there. I myself am showing off my interior designs."

"Charmaine," I said, remembering the old-fashioned tubular piece of metal I had pocketed at the murder scene last night, and van Dyne's comment about the decorator dabbling in stained glass, "do you know anything about light fixtures?"

"I purchase them, in consultation with various lighting designers."

"Who?"

She moved restlessly toward the door. "There are a number of them. Why?"

"I need someone to help light my apartment." Inwardly I grinned. My Mission District studio had sparkly things mixed in with the acoustical material on the ceiling, so I kept my lights as dim as possible.

"Oh." Charmaine paused, hand on the doorknob. "Try Victoriana. They're the biggest." In a cloud of exotic scent, she was gone.

"Thanks," I said, patting my bag where the piece of metal now rested. "Thanks. I will."

6

San Francisco Victoriana's showroom was in the industrial Bayshore District, several miles across town. I drove over there in a pensive mood, wondering if I were wasting my time pursuing this clue. It was, however, the only lead I had. The only lead except for Jake's comment about the person he was meeting being a drunk. If I interviewed all the drunks in a town like San Francisco, looking for a suspicious sign, I'd be at it for the rest of my life. No, better to try to track down the origin of the little piece of metal.

The showroom's walls were covered with plaster rosettes and fish-scale shingles like the ones Wintringham had pointed out on his family Queen Anne. From the ceiling hung dozens of light fixtures, their outstretched arms ending in etched-glass shades. I looked them over carefully as I waited at the sales desk, wondering how a piece of metal like the one in my purse would fit.

A gray cat lay curled on the desk. It raised its head and favored me with a great yawn. I scratched its ears, and it began to purr.

In a minute, a woman with short blond hair emerged from a room behind the desk. "Oh, I see you've met Victoria," she said cheerfully.

"Appropriately named."

"A little cutesy, but she's a cute cat. We've had her since she was a kitten. What can I do for you?"

"I need some information on light fixtures." I took out the metal piece. "I have a fragment of one here, and I'm trying to trace the manufacturer."

Her smooth brow creased. "Gosh, I don't know if I can help you. The guys who would know are at the home show." At my disappointed look, she added, "I'll give it a try, though. If it's somebody local, I might recognize it."

I handed her the fragment. She studied it, turning it over in her hands. Finally she said, "I could be wrong, but this looks like Prince Albert's work."

"Prince Albert!"

She grinned. "He's really Al Prince, but, like Victoria here, the name goes with the trade."

"Where might I find this royal personage?"

"His shop is on Natoma Street, that alley between Mission and Howard, south of Market. He's somewhere around Sixth. Look for a sign saying, 'Prince Albert's Lighthouse.' "

I thanked her and directed my battered red MG downtown.

Once there, I parked on Sixth Street, nicknamed "Rue de Wino" because of the characters with brown paper bags who hung out there. Natoma was one car wide, its sidewalks crowded with parked vehicles. I settled for the middle of the street, keeping alert for approaching motors.

I was not unfamiliar with this part of town, having worked cases here before, but now I was amazed to discover that people actually lived in the back alleys of this commercial district. The surrounding blocks consisted of stores, office buildings, and light industry, but here on a Saturday morning children played in the street, women hung laundry on porches, and men tinkered with old cars. The houses were largely wood frame and in bad repair. With my newfound knowledge, I recognized small squat Italianates and Sticks. The elegant Queen Anne, however, did not belong in this working-class neighborhood.

I continued along for two blocks, skirting abandoned tricycles and toys, until I saw the sign for Prince Albert's Lighthouse. It was a simple woodcarving that hung at a right angle to the face of the brick building. Another sign in the window said CLOSED.

Frustrated, I went up and peered in through the grimy plate glass. All I saw were worktables and unfamiliar machinery. A few light fixtures, similar to those at Victoriana, hung from the rafters.

The home show at Fort Mason—obviously that was the place to go. But first I had unfinished business to take care of. I returned to the MG and steered it toward Johnny's Kansas City Barbecue.

It was a mistake to appear there even at the tail end of the noon hour. I knew that as soon as I stepped in the door. Dark eyes in black faces turned toward me, and the level of noise dropped to a hush. Johnny Hart came forward, his face an angry mask.

"What the hell you doing here?" he demanded.

Summoning bravado, I said, "I thought I'd try some of your barbecued ribs."

"Well, forget it. Just get your ass out of here."

"Don't tell me you discriminate?"

"Sure I discriminate, 'specially against lying little sneaks."

"Don't you want to know why I asked all those questions last night?"

"I don't give a shit."

"Sure you do."

Exasperated, he looked around at his silent clientele. "All right, dammit. But we're not gonna talk here." He grabbed my elbow and propelled me toward the kitchen.

Inside were two waiters and a dishwasher. They looked up, startled, as we came in.

"You fellas get out there and take care of the customers, huh?" Hart said.

Puzzled, they exited to the front of the restaurant.

Hart leaned against a huge chopping block. "Lunchtime rush is almost over. So explain yourself, Miss Private Eye."

I blinked. "How'd you know?"

"I may be a nigger, girl, but I'm one of the literate ones. Your name's in the paper."

"Oh. Well, then you know why I asked you all that stuff."

"What I don't know is why the cover-up. You come around, you say, Look, I'm a private cop and this guy got dead—maybe I'll help you, maybe not. But I sure as shit won't lift a finger when you poke into things pretending to be some girlfriend of a knee-jerk liberal lawyer."

I grinned.

"What the hell's so funny?"

"You have just insulted Hank Zahn twice. Once by calling him a 'knee-jerk liberal' and once by implying he'd ever ask me out."

Hart tried to look stern, but a smile tugged at the corners of his mouth.

I looked around the kitchen, sniffing. "Sure smells good."

"So now you're trying to hit me up for a meal."

"All I've had today is coffee."

"Dammit, girl, I don't want to like you, and I don't want

to feed you, and I sense I'm gonna end up doing both. Ribs?"

"With fries."

"Beer?"

"Coke."

Hart went to the stainless-steel oven and threw some ribs on a plate, along with some greasy French fries from a vat of bubbling oil. While he was drawing my Coke, he said, "You still didn't explain yourself."

"It's really very simple: I wasn't on the case last night. I couldn't represent myself as investigating it without a client."

"So instead of this investigating, you snooped."

"I'm nosy, I guess."

He set the food in front of me. Ravenous, I dug in.

"So what do you want today?" Hart demanded. "You didn't come here to apologize for jiving me."

"Well, in a way," I said around a mouthful of fries. "I'm on the case now, and I need an ally in the community."

"On the case, huh? Who hired you?"

"David Wintringham."

"That fairy!"

"He's not so bad."

Sullenly, Hart shrugged.

"Well, he's not. Did you know his father?"

"There you go, pumping me again."

"It's my job."

"And you think I should help you with that job."

"Sure."

"What's in it for me?"

I sipped my Coke. "A good feeling deep down in your soul."

This time Hart grinned broadly. "You are the damndest. What do you want to know?"

"Richard Wintringham—what was he like?"

"Crazy old man." He stirred the big pot of barbecue sauce. "Lived up there in that big house all by himself. Strange man, but folks around here respected him. He gave the kids odd jobs, paid them good. Always sent a big load of food to the community center at Thanksgiving and Christmas. It was his neighborhood, and maybe he got off on being massa on the hill.''

"What about David Wintringham?''

"Checking up on your boss, huh?''

"You bet.''

Hart considered. "Now that's another kettle of fish entirely. Like I said, he's a fairy, and the old man didn't like that none.''

"Did he try to do anything about it?''

"Can't change a tiger's stripes. Oh, they fought some, I guess, but then the old man got killed, and David got it all. Right after, he moved to the house at the end of the block with his so-called friend, poor pudgy Paul.'' Hart smiled at his own alliteration.

"The police thought Richard Wintringham was killed by a burglar.''

Hart's eyes became veiled. "So I heard.''

I finished my ribs and scrubbed at my hands with a paper napkin. "But you didn't believe it. And you don't now.''

"What, you think you're a mind reader or something?''

"I'm right, aren't I?''

He sighed. "Maybe, maybe not. Folks around here knew Wintringham had a lot of valuable stuff in that house. But like I said, they respected him in a funny way. I think if it was a burglar that killed him, it wasn't anybody from the neighborhood. I would guess it was somebody from the outside.''

I couldn't quite credit that; junkies and rip-off artists had few loyalties. "Okay, Mr. Hart,'' I said, standing, "that's about all I need to know today. I take it I can come back if I have more questions?''

He shrugged.

"What do I owe you for lunch?''

"Forget it. It's on the house.''

"Well, thanks.''

"Don't mention it. I kind of like talking to you; keeps me on my toes. Only one thing.''

"Yes?"

"Next time you come, would you mind using the back door? Don't want to upset my clientele any more than I already have."

"I get it," I said and obliged by leaving that way. From the alley behind the building, I made a beeline for the phone booth that I'd called Greg and Hank from the night before. This time the lieutenant was in his office. He answered, sounding rushed.

"I wondered if you had the results of the postmortem on Jake Kaufmann," I said.

"Not yet, but we should by late afternoon. There've been two other murders, and we've got bodies stacked up in there like firewood, so they'll get it out fast."

No wonder he sounded harried. I chanced another request. "Greg, three years ago next month, another man was murdered in that house."

"Richard Wintringham. Right."

"Have you reviewed the file yet?"

There was a pause. "Who are you working for?"

"David Wintringham, the son."

"Jesus Christ, you can't keep out of it, can you?"

"No."

Another pause. I could picture him, drumming his fingers on the desk. "So now you want me to review the file on the Wintringham killing and pass along the details to you."

"Yes."

"Christ, papoose. . . . All right. I have to look it over anyway. Only let me tell you this: You and I are going to have a long, serious talk over dinner tonight."

"Greg, I may be sort of late for dinner." I had a few things I wanted to do first.

"How late?"

"Well . . ."

"Never mind. Why don't you meet me at my place whenever you can? That will give me the opportunity to entice you into my bed."

"All right."

"I don't believe it. You agreed."

"To the first, not the second."

"We'll see."

Maybe we would. It was a tempting prospect that had dangled between us for weeks. I said I'd see him later and hung up.

Outside the phone booth, I was startled by the specter of Johnny Hart, still in his stained chef's apron. He was out of breath.

"Got a message," he announced. "Nick Dettman wants to see you."

"Who's Nick Dettman?"

Hart looked outraged. "Who's Nick Dettman! Former city supervisor, big deal in this district, and you . . ."

"Now I remember him."

"Well, he wants to talk."

"When and where?"

"Tonight. He'll meet you at his law office on Haight Street at seven." He gave me the address. "You know where that is? Storefront with an orange door?"

I copied it down. "I'll find it."

"Good. I'll tell him you'll be there." Hart turned and loped off.

I watched him. Although I liked Johnny Hart, there was still—and probably always would be—a wary racial tension between us. Could I trust him? I didn't know.

Well, it looked like it would be an interesting evening on all fronts.

7

The lot at Fort Mason was jammed, so I had to park a long way from Pier Three. I hurried toward the waterfront, skirting cream-colored buildings with red roofs. The wide mouth of the pier gaped open, and people drifted in and out.

I'd been here a few years ago for the Dickens Christmas Fair, a yearly crafts-and-entertainment extravaganza. Then, the pier had been transformed into a scene straight out of Merrie Olde England; today the setting was more utilitarian. Rather than being concealed by pine boughs and Christmas lights, the ceiling arched to a peak, beams and pipes exposed. Rather than artful imitations of London shops, the booths were functional plywood structures. I started down one side, examining the exhibits.

From the Foundation for San Francisco's Architectural Heritage, I picked up a newspaper on local preservation efforts. The California Historical Society provided me with literature on its activities. The Preservation Group's booth featured color blowups of buildings it had restored for commercial use. I nodded familiarly at the chandeliers and cornice mouldings of Victoriana.

Halfway down, I came upon a familiar face. Charmaine. The little Japanese woman had obviously worked hard on her display. Rich purple velvets were draped against flowered wallpapers. Blue ceramic tiles in a fleur-de-lis pattern gleamed against paint samples in contrasting tones. Porcelain knickknacks sat atop spindly-legged tables. The effect was striking.

Charmaine spotted me, and her face crinkled into a smile. "So you decided to come to the show! Was Victoriana able to help you with your lighting problem?"

I started, realizing I'd half-forgotten my tale about wanting to light my apartment. "Sort of. Actually they referred me to someone else, a Prince Albert."

"Ah, Al. That was good of them; he can use the business."

"Is he here today?"

"Yes." She pointed to the opposite side of the pier.

"Then I think I'll go talk to him."

"Good. Enjoy the show."

I continued my leisurely journey around the pier, stopping when I came to Wintringham and Associates' booth. Like the Preservation Group's, it featured literature and color photographs of various projects. A young man hurried forward. His face, under a thatch of sandy hair, was moonlike, his body layered in unshed baby fat. I recalled Johnny Hart's comment about "poor pudgy Paul." This must be Wintringham's lover.

"Hello, I'm Paul Collins," the young man said, confirming my suspicion. "Are you thinking of buying a Victorian?"

"I'm afraid my paycheck won't allow it. Is David around?"

"No, he's not. Can I help you?"

"I'm Sharon McCone, the investigator he hired to look into Jake Kaufmann's death."

"Oh." Collins paled and put a hand to his forehead. "Such an awful business. It has me absolutely rattled and. . . . Jake dead in one of our houses. But what are you doing here? Surely you don't expect to find a murderer at a home show."

It was not as absurd as he made it sound. "Just getting to know the territory," I said with a conspiratorial wink.

Surprisingly, he returned it. "Well, if you need to see David, he'll be here in about an hour. Right now I'm the only one on the booth. Larry French was supposed to help, but he's off promoting something or other." Collins glanced around aggrievedly. "He's never where he should be and, really, this thing about Jake has me very upset."

I sensed a penchant for gossip here and encouraged it. "Did you know Jake well?"

"Pretty well, although not for very long. You see, he'd painted some of our previous restorations, and we'd just signed him to a contract to do the entire Steiner Street block. Before that he'd worked for David's father and done some spectacular houses on his own. We were really pleased to get him."

So, as I'd suspected, Jake had worked for Wintringham, Senior. "Who will paint the houses now?"

"Maybe Jake's assistants will carry on. It all depends on whether they can handle the conceptual work—the color design. And, of course, whether his widow will want to keep the business going."

"Did Jake plan to have a booth here today?"

"Oh, yes. It's right there at the end of the pier." Collins gestured vaguely. "His assistants are manning it. Jake would have wanted that."

"I'll take a look at it."

"Do that. I'll tell David you were by. And, if you see Larry, please tell him to get back here and help out."

I nodded and started off. Jake Kaufmann's booth was one of the more spectacular displays: a scaled-down replica of a Stick-style facade painted in Wedgewood blue, with accents of white and gold and deeper blues. Two men with longish hair were conversing with the spectators. I waited until the crowd drifted on, then went up and introduced myself.

"Oh, hey, I remember when you did that investigation for Jake," one of the assistants, with a Fu-Manchu moustache, said. "I'm Bob, and this is Ron." He pointed to his clean-shaven companion.

"What'll happen to the business now?" I asked.

Bob shrugged. "We'll keep it going. Both of us picked up a lot of know-how from Jake, and we want to make a go of it. Mrs. Kaufmann's already said she wants that too. She's one hell of a tough lady, got a lot of guts."

"Good for her. Listen: Did either of you notice anything strange about Jake's behavior yesterday?"

They exchanged troubled glances. Bob, who seemed to be the spokesman, asked, "Like what do you mean?"

"Did he seem worried? Upset? Afraid of something?"

Bob wet his lips. "Upset, maybe. He came out to a job we were on in the Haight, but he didn't check as thoroughly as he usually did, and he was pretty short with both of us."

"What time was this?"

"Maybe around three."

"That's a funny thing in itself." Ron spoke for the first time. "Jake usually came by in the morning, never later than one in the afternoon. I remember I wondered where he was."

"What about the day before?" I asked. "You notice anything strange then?"

Again they exchanged glances. Ron shook his head.

"Everything was like usual," Bob said.

So whatever had frightened Jake was a recent development. I told the painters I'd be in touch and continued on toward Prince Albert's booth. Before I reached it, however, the name SALVATION INCORPORATED stopped me. Eleanor van Dyne sat at a card table passing out literature. The rings on her fingers flashed as she spoke animatedly with the takers. I went up and waited my turn.

"Mrs. van Dyne?"

"Yes?" She looked up, patting her gray-blond coif.

"I doubt you remember me. My name is Sharon McCone. I investigated your charges against Jake Kaufmann."

"Of course I remember you." Her eyes narrowed, creating a network of fine wrinkles. "You're the young woman who went about annoying my neighbors when Jake committed that atrocity upon a perfectly decent Queen Anne row house across the street."

"I was only doing my job."

"Of course you were. You'd have been a fool to do otherwise. Actually, the stuffed shirts in my neighborhood were excited by a visit from a private detective, and a female one at that. It did them worlds of good, I daresay. I suppose you've heard about Jake?"

"As a matter of fact, I found his body."

"Good gracious!" She put a bejeweled hand to her throat. "What a grisly business! Why would a young woman of your looks and apparent intelligence want to involve herself in such sordid goings-on?"

"It beats sitting behind a desk shuffling paper."

She studied me for a moment. "Yes, I expect it does."

I doubted that Eleanor van Dyne had ever faced the choice I'd made between the humdrum jobs available to a sociology major and an occupation that, while low-paying, long-houred, and sometimes dangerous, fulfilled an inner craving for excitement. Avoiding her inquiring eyes, I looked down at the literature on the table. A colorful sheet advertised a house tour, co-sponsored by Salvation Incorporated and Heritage. It would culminate in a wine-and-cheese tasting at the Haas-Lilienthal house, headquarters of the latter.

"Are you interested in Victorians?" van Dyne asked, following my gaze.

"Yes, as a matter of fact I am." I took a breath and plunged into a bald-faced lie. "You see, I plan to buy and restore one I've found in the Western Addition."

"And I suppose you'll insist on one of those abominable psychedelic paint jobs?"

"Oh, no." I shook my head solemnly. "I liked Jake Kaufmann, you understand, but I didn't like what he was doing. I hold a much more traditional view of restoration."

As I'd hoped, van Dyne's eyes glittered at such a find. "Then perhaps you would enjoy this tour tomorrow. The houses included are classic examples of Victorians, and I plan to lead it myself. It will be at two in the afternoon, and I would be delighted to have you as my personal guest."

I smiled. "Why, thank you so much! I'll be there."

Van Dyne turned to the person beside me, and, pocketing the information sheet on the tour, I crossed to Prince Albert's booth.

Light fixtures similar to those at Victoriana hung from its latticed ceiling, and table lamps stood on makeshift shelves. Some had etched-glass globes, others little fluted shades, and still others were of colored glass in the Tiffany tradition. While they were obviously of modern manufacture, they had a strong aura of authenticity. In the center of the display, perched on a high stool, sat a wiry young man in a gray velvet frock coat and matching top hat with curling red plumes. A shock of ginger-colored hair stuck out from under the hat. This had to be Prince Albert.

"What can I do for you, milady?" he called out.

"I have a question. Victoriana said you might provide the answer."

"I have many answers. Come in, and take a seat on my

throne." He got up and, bowing, doffed his top hat toward the stool. His flowery speech and mannerisms completed his princely act, which was a little too cute for my taste.

"Don't mind if I do." I climbed up there and fished in my bag for the metal fragment. "I need to locate the manufacturer of this." I handed it to him.

His face underwent a transformation, wide mouth pulling down and eyes clouding. "Where did you find it?"

"In an empty house." I waved my hand vaguely.

"An empty house."

"Yes."

He stood close to me, tossing the metal piece from hand to hand. "I didn't introduce myself. I'm Al Prince, known in the trade as Prince Albert. Who're you?"

It wouldn't do any good to conceal my identity. He could ask any one of a number of people here, and chances were he'd seen my name in the newspaper this morning. I admitted who I was and my connection with the Kaufmann killing.

"So you must have found this in the empty house with Jake's body." Prince Albert stared at the fragment in his open palm, as if he could read the past from it. Then he shook his head. "Doesn't look familiar."

"Oh." I held out my hand.

He gave the fitting to me. Then abruptly he spun around. "Let's go outside. I can leave the booth for a while." He led me through one of the big side doors to the boardwalk next to the building. In the distance was the Golden Gate Bridge and the sailboats that dotted the Bay.

Prince Albert turned right, toward Alcatraz. We walked along slowly. The sunlight felt warm on my shoulders, and smells of creosote and seawater rose to my nostrils. Prince Albert didn't speak until we'd rounded the end of the pier, where fishermen were casting their lines. They leaned on the rail, their jackets hung over the stanchions, timeless figures far removed from the organized chaos inside the building. When we turned down the shady side where the wind whipped cruelly, Prince Albert finally said, "What makes you think that fitting is from a light fixture?"

"It had a broken bulb screwed into it, which I removed for safety's sake."

He nodded. "It's probably cast off an older fixture—from its shape I'd place it at late nineteenth century."

"But it's relatively modern?"

"Yes." He leaned his elbows on the railing, staring down into the green water. I did the same. Off to the left, a harbor cruise loaded with bundled-up tourists churned back to port.

"That piece isn't from one of your fixtures, then?" I persisted.

"I told you, no."

"And you have no idea whose it might be?"

"It's fairly typical. It could be anyone's."

We were silent for a moment, the wavelets lapping below.

"What does this fitting have to do with Jake's murder?" Prince Albert asked suddenly.

"I don't know. I hoped you could tell me."

He jerked around to face me. His eyes were hazel, flecked with yellow. "Why me?"

"You know your light fixtures, I'm told."

"Oh." He looked away.

"Did you know Jake?" I asked.

"We were friends."

"Good friends?"

"Good enough. He was like an older brother, gave me pointers on running my business."

"When was the last time you saw him?"

He was silent.

"When?" I insisted.

"Yesterday around noon, he was in my workshop."

"Why?"

"Just to talk."

"About what?"

"Inflation. The high price of liquor. What the hell *do* friends talk about?"

"How did he seem?"

"Seem?"

"What kind of mood was he in?"

"His usual."

"And that was . . ."

Prince Albert sighed explosively. "He was the same as he always was. He was like Jake, that's all." He paused, then added, "Let me see that fitting again, will you?"

I passed it to him. He took it, fumbled, and said, "Oops!" He straightened. The metal piece had flipped from his hand and dropped into the green water below.

He turned to me, mock dismay twisting his wide mouth. "How clumsy of me!"

Fury rose, but I controlled it. I didn't want him to think his artifice a triumph. "Very clumsy, for a man who does intricate work with his hands."

"I hope I haven't hindered your investigation."

"Not at all," I replied smoothly. "I took pictures of the piece last night." I hadn't, but I was sure I could sketch it from memory.

Chagrin flickered across his face, but he smiled. "Well, that's a relief. I must make it up to you, though."

"And how do you propose to do that?"

"Come by my shop tomorrow morning, before noon, when I have to be out here. I'll give you the background on the fixture trade, show you how they're cast. Maybe that will help, even if I have lost your . . . er . . . clue."

And in the meantime, he would pump me about my investigation. Still, I might take him up on it. I'd keep my guard up—more, certainly, than I had today. And perhaps I'd find out something about Prince Albert. "Thank you. It will be a pleasure."

With a courtly gesture, Prince Albert offered me his velvet-clad arm. I took it, and we continued down the shady side of the pier.

8

Halfway back to my car, I saw a familiar figure lumbering toward the gate. "Paul!" I called. "Paul Collins!"

The pudgy young man turned, puzzled, then raised a hand in greeting. I quickened my pace and joined him.

"How come you're leaving so early?" I asked. It wasn't quite five, and the show would continue until nine.

"David arrived, and Larry's there. With more than two people, the booth is crowded." His moonlike face drooped. "Besides, if you want the truth, I'm not feeling very well. That murder . . ."

"Do you need a ride? I have my car."

He brightened slightly. "Thanks, I *could* use one. The bus service in our neighborhood. . . . Well, you hate to ride them. With those teenage thugs holding up the passengers . . ."

Already I sensed Collins was a man who rarely completed a sentence, as if he had second thoughts on the worth of what he had to say. We walked in silence to the MG, and I waited as he squeezed his plump body into the passenger seat.

"If the neighborhood's so bad," I said as I drove out of the lot, "why do you stay there?"

"It's David's home."

"Don't you have any say about where you live?"

He looked surprised, as if the prospect had never occurred to him. "I suppose I would, if I bothered. But it's much easier to go along with what David wants, since it means so much to him."

"Why does it?"

"He's very attached to the family mansion."

"The big Queen Anne on the corner."

"Yes, the one where . . ." He stared out the window.

"Does he plan to live there when it's restored?"

"He did. Now . . ." Collins groped in his jacket pocket and

produced a pill bottle. He poured two yellow tablets into his
hand and gulped them. "Valium," he explained. "For neck tension, but today they help other kinds."

I nodded sympathetically.

"I don't know what David will do about the house now,"
Collins went on. "I could never understand his . . . well, I hate
to call it an obsession, but it borders on that. Sure, Victorians are
nice, I guess, but. . . . Where I come from—Dayton, Ohio—we
have big old houses too, but you don't see all the fuss."

Dayton, Ohio. So Paul Collins was one of the legion of
homosexuals who had fled the Midwest to find freedom and
acceptance in San Francisco. I glanced at him as he sat, gripping
his knees with his hands and staring rigidly ahead. A complaint
of neck tension was an easy way to get a prescription for tranquilizers, and I was willing to bet there was nothing wrong with
Collins' neck. He probably took Valium because he hadn't yet
come to terms with emerging from the closet. It was not surprising, given Dayton, Ohio.

I could well understand his discomfort. Look at my own
background: Would the high-school cheerleader and navy brat
from conservative San Diego have believed that, as an adult, she
would not only tolerate what she then knew as "homos," but also
include a few among her circle of friends? And yet even now,
wasn't I, truthfully, uncomfortable when conversations with
those friends turned to the details of gay life? Nine years in the
Bay Area had changed me, but the vestiges of twenty in San
Diego still clung.

I pulled up in front of the houses on Steiner Street. Collins
still sat gripping his knees. He turned to me and said earnestly,
"They *are* pretty houses. I just don't understand this obsession
. . ."

I felt much the same way. While I was not indifferent to the
Victorians' charms, I preferred the clean, sleek lines of contemporary architecture. But that was me: Why take a train when you
can fly? Why figure by hand when you can use a computer?

To Collins, I said, "You're not required to share others'
enthusiasms."

He smiled at the words of support. "I guess. Look, would you like to come up for some tea? I have fresh scones, from the bakery on Union Street."

The idea appealed to the Scot in me, as well as to my stomach. I accepted his invitation and followed him up the stairway to the yellow-and-blue house.

"Come to the kitchen. That's my domain." Collins led me through the double doors and dining room to a kitchen that was streamlined in every detail. Stainless-steel appliances gleamed. Gadgets for every possible purpose stood on the butcher-block counters. At the rear, sliding glass doors opened onto a redwood deck with bright lawn furniture. The kitchen was spotless, artfully arranged. I reflected that it would fit with Collins' personality to be compulsively neat.

The suspicion was borne out by the precision with which he set the table, lining up red stoneware and Danish flatware on geometrically patterned placemats. He motioned for me to sit while he busied himself with teakettle, scones, and jam.

"How long have you lived in San Francisco?" I asked.

He poured tea and sat opposite me. "Four years, almost. I came out with David a couple of years after I graduated from college."

"Where did you meet him?"

"In New York. I'd inherited some money and gone there because I was interested in the theater, but I was having a hard time breaking in. I don't know how familiar you are with the gay scene."

"Reasonably."

"Then you know it can get pretty, well . . . rough. I'm a conservative guy, and the kinkier side of it isn't for me. And it can get lonely, too. It's hard to meet people. I guess it's the same for any single person, but . . ."

I nodded. I'd had my fair share of difficulty meeting men, although my work brought me into contact with more of them than the average job.

"Well, I was about to give up and go home when I met

David. He was ten years older than me, an engineer, with a good job. I could look up to him, depend on him. And David . . . well, I guess he needed a home."

I looked around the spotless kitchen. Indeed Collins provided that. My eyes lit on a large portable TV set rolled into a corner. When I looked at Collins, he was blushing.

"My vice," he admitted. "I like to watch TV while I cook, especially crime shows. That was why I wanted to talk to you—it fascinates me, meeting a private eye."

I grinned. "If only you knew how boring it can be. Some of our clients find the most humdrum reasons for taking legal action. And, speaking of clients, what's David like? I haven't talked with him enough to know."

Collins tilted back his chair, brown eyes thoughtful. "I'd describe him first of all as intense. He gets wrapped up in his projects, he can't sit down, he zips around burning up these fantastic amounts of energy. You should see him on a job site. He's always peering over the workmen's shoulders, crawling on the scaffolding, pitching in to help. It tires me out to watch him."

"Was he close to his father?"

The non sequitur startled Collins. "Why do you ask?"

"He mentioned his father this morning."

"Oh." Collins studied his plump hands. "I'd say it was an ambivalent relationship."

"How so?"

"Mr. Wintringham was a very controlling person. Don't get me wrong, he was also a nice man. I liked him, but. . . . David was already a grown man in his thirties when we came back from New York, but his father tried to dominate his life."

"Did David resist?"

"To a certain extent. You can probably guess his father wasn't too happy about us. When David and I got here, we lived separately for a while, but we started restoring this house right away, and David made it clear that we would move in here together. And Mr. Wintringham didn't approve when David started Wintringham and Associates, but he went ahead with it anyway. All in all, he resisted pretty well, but I know it was hard for him. Deep down, he loved his father and felt guilty because he hadn't lived up to his expectations."

"What were they, besides being heterosexual?"

Collins crumbled a piece of scone on his plate. "He wanted David to become an architect like him, but instead he studied engineering and even preferred construction work to that. When he became a general contractor, his father considered it . . . well, tacky, and . . ." The sound of footsteps distracted him.

The swinging door from the dining room burst open, and Charmaine confronted us. Her bell-like hair was disarrayed, her face contorted in fury. "Where is that son-of-a-bitch?" she demanded.

Collins' hands clenched. "Charmaine, what *is* wrong? Where is *who?*"

"You know damn well who! That slimy little bastard was supposed to wait for me at the show, but instead he took off in his goddamned Porsche with some blond. I let him have it, believe me I did, but he just walked out of there with her!" Her mouth trembled, and her eyes filled, washing out the anger.

"Oh, Charmaine." Collins held out an arm. "Come sit down and have some tea. That's how Larry operates. You should know by now."

She sat, elbows on the table, hair swinging forward to cover her face, and her tears.

So Larry French was the sleazy boyfriend van Dyne had mentioned. I should have known, from his treatment of Charmaine this morning. What an odd combination! Surely Charmaine could do better.

Collins poured tea into a fresh cup, making comforting sounds. I looked at my watch. There was half an hour before my seven o'clock appointment with Nick Dettman, but I decided I would walk over to his law offices to kill the time rather than intrude further upon Charmaine's distress.

9

At ten minutes to seven dusk had fallen. I had walked down Steiner and admired the old mansions around Alamo Square, but now I approached Haight Street, or more specifically, the five-hundred block of Haight, known as "The Razor" because of its thriving drug trade.

My hand tightened on the strap of my shoulder bag, and I walked in the center of the sidewalk, out of reach of both the buildings and the parked cars. I was state qualified in firearms and owned two .38 revolvers. Unlike many in my profession, I liked guns and practiced regularly at a firing range. I did not usually carry one, however, because all too often a gun could intensify an already dangerous situation. In spite of that conviction, tonight I longed for its comforting weight in my bag.

Black men lounged against the iron grilles of the storefronts. They congregated in the middle of the sidewalk, talking, gesturing, making deals. I could tell the pushers because they carried bottles of soda pop. A detective on the narcotics detail had once explained to me that the heroin was packaged in toy balloons and distributed out of apartments that were changed every few days. The soda pop was a normal precaution for the street dealers. Should the law appear, they would swallow the balloons, washing them down with pop. The balloons, of course, could be recovered later.

I made my way toward Nick Dettman's storefront. I had decided not to bring my car to this area, where autos seemed to disappear as soon as they were parked, but now I regretted it. Lewd remarks followed me. An occasional hand reached out. I weaved, silently avoiding them. Soon the loiterers were behind, and I spotted the orange door Johnny Hart had described.

Large gold letters on the plate-glass windows said: NICK

DETTMAN, ATTORNEY-AT-LAW. The room was brightly lit. I opened the door and stepped in.

A Formica counter ran across the front of the office, and sagging rattan furniture filled the waiting area. The rubber plant on the counter looked dusty and discontented. The place made All Souls seem on a par with the plushest Financial District tax firm. I saw no one.

A deep voice said, "Come all the way in, please, and close the door. We have to conserve heat."

I did so and went around the counter.

The owner of the voice sat at a desk toward the rear. He leaned back in his swivel chair, hands clasped on his paunch, little feet barely touching the floor. I recognized his lined black features and receding hairline from old newspaper photographs.

"Hello, Mr. Dettman," I said.

"Miss McCone." He nodded. "Please have a seat."

I took the chair opposite him and looked around the room. Framed photographs of Africans that looked like they'd been clipped from *National Geographic* decorated the walls. There were shelves of unpainted plywood, piled with reference books and papers.

"Not an elegant establishment, but we do the best with what we have." Dettman's speech was educated, with only a trace of the ghetto.

"Since I work for a legal-services plan, I understand that necessity."

"Yes, All Souls. A good group. I presume you know Hank Zahn."

"He's my boss, as much as anyone there is. Our organizational structure is loose, to say the least."

"Do tell him hello for me the next time you see him."

I nodded. Not only would I do that, but I would also pump Hank for details about Dettman.

Dettman unclasped his hands and slipped one finger under his striped tie, which was looped over but not knotted at the neck. Rhythmically he flapped it up and down, regarding me in silence.

"Mr. Dettman," I said after a moment, "you asked to see me. I assume you do have something to say."

"In good time." He continued to flap the tie. "Let me start with a few questions."

"Such as?"

"Who are you working for?"

"I don't have to tell you that."

"But it would make our conversation so much easier." The words were slow, measured. Instinctively I glanced over my shoulder.

"No, Miss McCone, we're quite alone."

I smiled, covering my nervousness. "Good. I like my discussions to be kept private. As to your question, you already know who I'm working for. There's no reason Johnny Hart wouldn't have told you. He hurried me through his restaurant so fast this noon that I didn't see you there, though."

It was a good guess, and it drew a thin smile from Dettman.

"So let's get down to business," I went on. "Why did you ask me here?"

The corners of his mouth turned down. He stopped flapping the tie, and his hand crept forward to his littered desk. I tensed, imagining a gun, then almost laughed when he pulled a Fig Newton from a cookie box resting there. He popped it whole into his mouth and chewed, cheeks puffed out.

Around the cookie, he said, "You're a forceful young woman, Miss McCone."

"In my business, one has to be. And, speaking of business, may I once again suggest we get down to it."

His hand strayed toward the cookie box, but he restrained it and laced his fingers over his paunch. "All right, Miss McCone," he said, "we'll begin with some background about this part of the city."

"The Western Addition, you mean?"

He shrugged. "Western Addition, Hayes Valley, Fillmore, call it what you will. Every mapmaker has a different label for it, and boundaries overlap. Let's go into its history.

"The Western Addition was a prime residential area in the eighteen seventies and eighties, when the fine old homes your friend Wintringham is so fond of were built. Many of them survived the earthquake of oh-six because the boundary line where they dynamited to stop the fire's spread was Van Ness Avenue, several blocks east of here. In fact, for a while after the 'quake, Fillmore Street was a major shopping area for the entire city."

"Interesting, but I don't see the relevance."

He unclasped his hands and began flapping the tie again. "Let me continue. During World War Two, the shipyard business flourished in San Francisco. Southern blacks flocked to this area by the thousands to find work. The old homes were broken up into flats, and the ghetto you see today was under way."

"So what Wintringham is doing should be a welcome change."

Dettman shook his head. "What do you know about our local population shifts, Miss McCone?"

"There's been an exodus from the city. The middle class, especially families with children, have fled to the suburbs. It's left us with the poor on one hand, the rich on the other, and a lot of single people somewhere in between who, like myself, prefer urban life."

"Your information is out of date."

"How so?"

"Recently there's been a return to the city, mainly by middle-class whites who couldn't take the suburbs. There's also been an influx of gays, who are well off as a rule because most gay households have two wage earners and no children. These people are moving into areas like the Western Addition, buying up old homes, and restoring them."

I remembered Johnny Hart's similar comments to Hank and

me last night. "And they're displacing the blacks who have lived here for generations."

"Right. Do you know where the next black ghettos will be?"

"No."

"In the older tracts of the suburbs. South, in Daly City. East, in Concord. Down the Peninsula. Look at East Palo Alto—as far back as twelve years ago, the residents sponsored an initiative on the ballot to change the name to Nairobi."

"Okay, I hear what you're saying. But, still, what does all this have to do with the murder I'm investigating?"

Dettman leaned forward, his palms flat on the desk. "It has everything to do with it. People don't like to be displaced, to have to move far from their jobs and the area they call home. There's a great deal of anger brewing in this neighborhood. We have a drug traffic that's run out of control. What you see here is an upsurge of rage. And when large numbers of people get angry, others get hurt."

"And you think Jake Kaufmann was a victim of that rage?"

"I know it."

I regarded him warily. There was a strange light in his eyes and his fingers, laced together once more, twitched. I wondered if Nick Dettman were completely sane.

"How do you know this, Mr. Dettman?"

"I know my neighborhood. I know my people."

"Or do you know about one specific person?"

"What?"

"Do you know who killed Jake Kaufmann?"

Our eyes locked together in the long silence. Then Dettman leaned back in his chair and gave a hollow laugh. "If I knew that, would I tell you?"

"No, but it doesn't hurt to ask."

"You'd be surprised, Miss McCone, how much it can hurt to ask. You can become one of the people damaged by the anger I described."

"Is that a threat?"

"Of course not. But you should realize that the streets around here aren't the safest place for a pretty white woman."

I didn't like Nick Dettman and I didn't like his insinuation. I stood up. "All right, if that's the level this conversation has sunk to, I'm going."

His hand crept toward the cookie box, and again he pulled it back. "You won't go before I give you a message for that faggot client of yours."

"Oh, yes?"

"You go back there and you tell him he'd better halt that housing project and get out of my neighborhood."

"Or else?"

He frowned.

"Or else?" I repeated. "When you threaten a person, there's always an 'or else.'"

His dark features twisted. It was a moment before he could speak. "Yes, Miss McCone, there is an 'or else.' People will get hurt. Like Jake Kaufmann was. It could start with Wintringham. Or his workers. Or his buddy, Paul. It could even start with you."

"Or you, Mr. Dettman," I replied quietly. "Or it could start with you."

I whirled and strode out of there, pausing briefly on the sidewalk to catch my breath. A young black man in a leather coat stepped around me, throwing me a puzzled glance. It wasn't until he had entered Dettman's orange door that I recognized him as the man who had come into Johnny Hart's the night before with the news of the "white dude's" murder.

10

Normally I would have waited outside to see what happened between the two men, but that would be foolhardy at night in this neighborhood. I hurried back to the Victorian block on Steiner Street by a more circuitous, but safer, route than I'd come.

Dim lights showed in the windows of the yellow-and-blue Italianate. I knocked and, when I received no response, tried the door. It was unlocked. Crossing the hallway to the parlor, I saw flickering light in the dining room. I went back there, calling out Wintringham's name.

Flames roared and leapt on the hearth of the fireplace. I stepped toward their warmth then turned, startled. Larry French sat at the long trestle table. A bottle of bourbon stood in front of him, the reflection of the flames playing on its surface. French nodded at me and tipped a glass to his lips.

"Davie-poo's not here, McCone." His speech, while not slurred, sounded like he'd had a lot to drink. Was French the habitual drunk I was looking for?

"Do you know when he'll be back?"

"After the show closes. Eight-thirty, nine."

I looked at my watch. It was close to that now.

French removed his feet from the chair where they'd been propped. "You're welcome to wait, if you can stand being in the same room with me. I'll even offer you a drink."

"I can use one."

"Fetch yourself a glass." He indicated the built-in cabinets on the far wall.

I chose one from a collection of crystal. French produced ice from a silver bucket and poured, almost to the brim.

"Has it often been your experience that people can't stand

to be in the same room with you?" I asked, sitting.

"Tonight it has." French refilled his own glass, not bothering with ice.

"Who?"

"You don't really care."

"It's as good a way as any to kill time." Besides, Wintringham's pug-faced business partner interested me. I was certain I'd heard of him before, but I couldn't place where.

"Yeah, I always heard private dicks were nosy and, being a woman, I guess you're doubly so."

I fixed him with a stern gaze.

"Aaaah, don't glare at me. I've taken enough shit tonight from Charmaine."

I recalled the decorator's distraught state. "She bawl you out for leaving her at the show?"

"Oh, you already heard. My fame spreads fast. Well, shit, she had her own car. And this chick needed a ride. Christ, McCone, Charmaine raised a big stink at the show and then when I got back here she wanted to start in again. What's the matter with you broads anyway? Get you in the sack a few times and you think you own a guy."

I bit back harsh words. Arguing wouldn't get me any information. "So Charmaine is just a casual lay to you?"

"They're all casual. When you've been around the business as long as I have, you learn to keep it that way."

"The construction business?"

He flashed me an exasperated look and gulped his drink. "No, McCone, not the construction business. The entertainment business. Don't you know who I am?"

"No."

"Ignorant, McCone, ignorant. I'm *the* Larry French. Promoter. Rock concerts. You heard of me. I made Bill Graham look like peanuts once."

I had heard of him, but years ago. "You sponsored a lot of big tours. What happened?"

"It got to be a pain in the ass, that's what happened. I took my bread and put it to work for me, instead of working for it."

"Like with this project?"

"This one I've been in on for a year, and before that plenty of other investments. I'm diversified. And I don't do a lick of work. Oh, I run around here to the job sites, make sure the workers know I've got my eye on them. But that's strictly a pastime. I don't give a shit about construction."

"Nice. I wouldn't mind such easy work myself."

"Yeah, you would."

"Why?"

His little eyes were shrewd in spite of the alcohol. "Because, McCone, you're the kind who gets a kick out of what you do. You're nosy, and you like to play tough, and you probably have some half-assed idea you're making the world a better place— only you don't own up to that."

I felt a twinge of discomfort at the way he had me pegged. But, then, I also had him pegged. Larry French hadn't retired from the entertainment business because it had become a "pain in the ass." Not him—his type liked being in the limelight, wheeling and dealing, rubbing elbows with the stars. I wondered about the real reason he had bowed out, and decided I'd have to unearth it.

The front door opened, and French looked up, bored with me, already hoping for a new face. I turned and saw David Wintringham.

"Hi, Larry. Sharon, don't tell me you have something to report?"

I'd decided not to tell him about Nick Dettman's threat until I could check up on the black man and assess how serious he might be. "Nothing concrete. I need more information from you."

"Sure. Let me get a glass of wine, and I'll join you."

French and I sipped our drinks in silence, waiting for Wintringham to return. He did, sprawling on a chair across from me and placing the jug of red wine between us. "What do you need to know?"

"Let's start with this project. Is it in solid shape?"

He rubbed his nose. "We've got adequate financial backing."

"Mine," French put in.

"Is the work progressing on schedule?"

"Well, there've been some setbacks."

French snorted.

Wintringham said, "Larry sees them as far more serious than they are. He's not all that familiar with how this business works."

"Business is business. A six-month halt is serious."

"Will you let me tell this!" Wintringham snapped.

French shrugged and poured himself more bourbon. Obviously he had a good head for liquor, better than mine, which was not bad. I slid my glass farther away from me, remembering my appointment with Greg.

"The setbacks," Wintringham said, "are standard. Trouble getting permits. Hassles with City Planning."

"And vandalism," French added. "We put in a window, some kid heaves a brick through it. Slogans sprayed on freshly painted walls: 'Kill the Pigs. Faggots Go Home.' "

"That's typical of any project in a fringe area," Wintringham said.

French wasn't to be stopped. "Then there're the workmen who show up with six beers on their breath at ten in the morning and leave by three."

"That happens with nonunion labor," Wintringham said. "But nonunion labor saves money. And they're not all like that. You fired the worst one last week."

"After I caught him sitting on the scaffolding smoking a joint."

I said, "Given your background, I wouldn't have thought that would bother you."

"Look, McCone, a singer smokes a J or snorts some coke to get up there, then goes on stage and gives one hell of a performance. That's one thing. But some goddamned handyman gets stoned, falls off the scaffolding, and next thing we're up to our asses in insurance claims. You follow?"

"I follow." I turned back to Wintringham. "I take it the project is under way again?"

"We have the permits," he said grimly. "It's going."

French raised a skeptical eyebrow and drained his glass.

"What about your prospects for selling these houses?" I asked. "Don't you anticipate difficulty, given the neighborhood?"

"We've been restoring and reselling for three years now. We've had no trouble."

"Where were your other restorations?"

He shifted uncomfortably in his chair. "Well, the Haight. Noe Valley."

"But never this area before."

"No."

"So you very well may have problems, given the junkies and proximity to public housing projects."

He sipped his wine. "Okay, granted, we may."

"Do you know of anyone who wants to put a stop to the project?"

"Eleanor van Dyne. But I already told you that."

"Anyone else?"

He glanced at French, who asked, "What are you getting at, McCone?"

"Just digging."

"Nosy broad."

I understood why Wintringham didn't let French's remarks irk him. Pure ritual, they were already sailing past me. "What about you, French? Do you have any enemies from your rock-and-roll days who might want to hurt you financially?"

"Anybody who's anybody in the business has enemies, but I doubt mine would get back at me by clobbering a house painter I'd hired."

He was probably right. And I couldn't see van Dyne, in all her elegance, doing Jake in. Still, I'd have to check her out.

"All right," I said, "now let's talk about your father's murder, David. The police theorized a burglar killed him. What was taken?"

"Small valuable things. Things that would have been easy to carry. . . . Paul, how are you feeling?"

Paul Collins appeared in the archway from the parlor. He wore a plaid bathrobe and slippers, and his sandy hair was tousled. "Better, thanks. I heard voices."

"We're going over some things with Sharon. Do you want a glass of wine?"

"Yes, I'd like that." Collins poured from the jug. I wondered if drinking were wise on top of the Valium he'd taken. Well, Collins must know his capacity.

"Tell me about the things that were taken," I said to Wintringham.

"What things?" Collins asked.

"The ones that were stolen the night of Dad's murder."

"Oh." Collins gulped wine.

Wintringham tilted back in his chair. "Let me see. There were a few pressed-glass bottles and flasks; Dad had a collection of those. A porcelain vase from the Ming Dynasty. A small mantel clock. A very rare silver hot-water kettle. And, of course, the Cheshire Cat's Eye."

"The what?"

Collins said, "David, are you sure it's good for you to relive all this?"

"If it will help Sharon solve Jake's murder."

"But, David . . ." Collins poured more wine. "This is a different murder entirely, and I don't see—"

"Neither do I," French put in, "but if he wants to spend his money and McCone's time on some half-assed idea, let him."

"But it upsets him to talk—"

"Paul." Wintringham held up a hand. "Be quiet and drink your wine. I'm not upset."

Sulkily, Collins nodded and sipped.

"The Cheshire Cat's Eye," Wintringham went on, "was a Tiffany lamp, commissioned in nineteen hundred by my grandfather as a gift for his newborn son, my father."

"Describe it."

"It was a nursery lamp. The base was bronze, and it resembled a tree trunk, with the branches spreading out at the top, under the shade."

"But why was it called the Cheshire Cat's Eye?"

"Because of the design of the shade. It was the leaves of a tree, with the Cheshire Cat grinning through them. The leaves were in autumn colors: red, brown, and gold. The teeth were iridescent white, a big grin. And the eye—Tiffany departed from the popular conception of the cat by giving it only one eye. He also departed from his usual technique of exclusively using glass by making the eye a greenish-yellow gemstone, appropriately called cat's-eye."

"And the lamp was used in your father's nursery?"

"Yes, in the big Queen Anne. As he grew up, my grandfather read him *Alice in Wonderland* and told him a fanciful tale about how the Cheshire Cat had come to live in the special lamp in our house. Later, my father passed the story on to me."

It was fascinating, made more so by the tubular piece of metal that had sunk irretrievably into the Bay this afternoon.

"Was the lamp electric?" I asked.

"Kerosene."

Odd . . .

Collins groaned, and Wintringham looked at him with concern.

"I think I've had too much wine," the pudgy man said.

"How much Valium did you take today?" Wintringham demanded.

"Quite a lot. I was upset . . ."

"Then you shouldn't drink at all. We'd better get you right upstairs to your room."

Collins nodded and both men rose. "Excuse us, please," Wintringham said.

I stood too. "That's okay. I'm already late for an appointment."

French remained seated, watching them leave, a smirk on his pug-like face. "Nice little couple, huh, McCone? Poor pudgy

Paul and his tranquilizers and motherly David and his T.L.C.''

"Mr. French," I said, "if you dislike everything and everyone here so much, why do you hang around?"

"Beats working." He continued to stare in the direction they'd gone, his face thoughtful now. "And sometimes you figure out some damned interesting things."

"Such as?"

"No way, McCone. You do your own figuring. I'll do mine."

11

Greg set two glasses of white wine on the low table in front of our easy chairs. Beyond it, a fire smoldered on the hearth. The same adjective could also be applied to Greg's mood. I wondered if he were about to burst into flame or cool down like the logs.

I sipped the wine and avoided his eyes, first glancing toward the windows that usually presented a Twin Peaks panorama of the city. Unfortunately, the draperies were closed. I then directed my gaze out the French doors, where floodlights played on a garden that cascaded down the steep slope of the hill. How long I could feign fascination with its vines and shrubs I didn't know, but they were preferable to Greg's grim countenance.

"Think you'll find a clue out there?"

I jerked my head toward where he sat in the companion chair at my side. "What?"

"That's where you've been all evening, chasing after clues, isn't it?"

"Greg, I've already apologized for being late." And not all that late; I'd arrived a little after ten.

"I don't care about the time. I'm capable of amusing myself while waiting for you."

"Then what the hell is wrong?"

"What is wrong is that you are messing around with matters that in no way concern you." He spoke very slowly and precisely.

I felt a flash of anger. "David Wintringham hired me. It's my job."

"Your job, as I understand it, is staff investigator for All Souls. It consists of interviewing prospective witnesses, researching public records, and—"

"And occasionally tracking down killers!"

His dark eyebrows shot up sardonically. "And how often do you perform this function?"

Trying to keep cool, I sipped some wine and choked. As I doubled over, coughing, Greg patted me on the back. His touch was not all that gentle. Recovering, I said, "My job is to provide any investigative services our clients require."

"Like I said, how many murderers have you tracked down?"

I glared at him.

"Well?"

"Two," I replied sullenly.

"Yeah. Not a bad average, but the first time you almost got yourself killed. The second time, you almost lost a friend."

"Nonsense. I—"

He grabbed my right hand. "You see that scar?"

Unwillingly I looked down at the souvenir of my first murder case. "I know it's there. You don't have to remind me. But it certainly wasn't a fatal—"

"That knife could have pierced you in lots worse places."

"I know that too."

He dropped my hand and I reached for my wineglass. "I have some additional information for you," I said, trying not to sound grudging.

"Oh?"

"It's something Jake said to me on the phone, something I'd forgotten."

"What?"

"He said that the person he was meeting was unreliable because he had a drinking problem."

"He?"

"Figure of speech. Actually, I think he said 'the person.' Anyway, I don't think it counts for much, because I haven't come across anyone who drinks to that degree. Of course, the person could be a closet drinker."

"Also, this person may not have been his killer."

"Maybe, but it seems logical."

"Logic! Like I've said before about your logic—"

"Well, for what it's worth—and I agree that it's probably not much—that's what he said."

"Thanks. I'll make a note of it."

"And now," I added, "in exchange tell me the results of Jake's postmortem."

Greg rolled his eyes at the ceiling. "Give me patience, oh lord!"

"Please, Greg."

"You don't know when to quit!"

"Damned right I don't!"

We sat, stubborn glares locked. Would we ever be together more than an hour without getting into a verbal tug-of-war? I doubted it.

Finally Greg shrugged and settled back in his chair, glass in hand. "The cause of death," he began, "was a blow to the mastoid bone, which resulted in a severe cranial hemorrhage. I won't bore you with the technical details."

I ignored the latter comment. It could be a cheap shot, or it could be that Greg himself considered the details boring. "Did they fix the time of death?"

"Around eight P.M."

"And I got there shortly before nine. He had asked me to meet him at seven-thirty, so that means the killer either was to be part of that meeting or knew about it."

"Possibly."

"And the accident definitely was faked?"

"Yes. Besides the factors you observed, when the body was moved we found very little paint under it. Had he fallen from the ladder and knocked the can over with him, there would have been more. It looks as if it were poured on and around him."

I sighed with relief, and Greg looked at me oddly. I kept silent, not wanting to reveal the contents of last night's bad dreams: Jake unconscious and drowning in the viscous liquid.

"What about other evidence at the scene? Any fingerprints?"

"The ladder, brush, and paint can were wiped clean. Your prints were nice and clear. The others will be checked, but chances are they'll either be partials or turn out to belong to workmen."

"And the murder weapon?"

"The injury was consistent with the shape of an ordinary hammer."

"Did you find it?"

With an irritated motion, he crushed out his half-smoked cigarette. "No. We've combed the area, but there were plenty of hammers around the construction sites. The lab will have to test them all, and that'll take time. And, in the end, the killer probably took it with him and disposed of it where it will never turn up."

I nodded, my mind on the metal piece I'd snatched up. "Anything else interesting at the scene?"

He turned to face me. "What do you have in mind?"

"Oh, I noticed a lot of debris."

"Most of which had been torn out of the house in the restoration process."

"There was some colored glass."

"Yes, there was."

"Well, was that from the house?"

His eyes narrowed. "It may have been."

"Could you tell if it was . . . you know, old?"

He paused, gazing intently at my face. "Sharon, is there something you want to tell me?"

"I don't understand."

"Yes, you do."

"Greg, all I asked was a simple question about something I noticed at the murder scene."

"Hmmm. Yes. I see."

"*Was* the glass old?"

He relented. "No. It was standard modern glass, plus portions of a light bulb. The lab did a spectrographic analysis." My face must have fallen, because Greg frowned and repeated, "Are you sure you don't have something I should know?"

I thought of the tubular metal piece and my negligence in letting it out of my hands. A wave of guilt washed over me. Admit I'd taken evidence from a murder scene and lost it? Never, not to Greg. "I wish I did. So far, all I've come up with are a number of peculiar characters." Briefly, I described them, omitting Dettman's threat.

When I'd finished, Greg said, "Well, I'm sure your path is crossing those of my men. Try to keep out of their way, will you? We've got two other new murders to deal with, and we're shorthanded."

"Don't worry." Irritated, I silently vowed to get far ahead of his plodding investigators.

Greg relaxed in his chair again, head resting on the high back. There were tired lines on his face, and I felt a flash of sympathy. Three new murders was a big case load, even for a man with as much energy as the lieutenant, and I didn't want to press him further, but I still needed to know about the Richard Wintringham file.

Assuming a casual pose, I sipped wine and said, "Oh, by the way, did you get a chance to go over the file on that old murder?"

He sighed. "If tenacity wasn't one of the things I admire most about you, I'd boot you out of here for that. Yes, I looked at it."

"And?"

"It appears to have been a simple case of murder in the course of a burglary. A servant found the old man in his study in the tower room on the second floor. Wintringham had been bludgeoned to death late the previous evening."

"Like Jake Kaufmann."

"Like him, but don't make too much of it."

"What about alibis?"

"Who did you have in mind?"

"Well, the son, David Wintringham."

"Trusting of your client, aren't you? David was at home, and his lover, Paul Collins, backed that up the same as this time. Everyone we interviewed in connection with the case had a good alibi, which gives further credence to the burglary theory."

"Did any of the objects taken ever turn up?"

"No. We circularized, of course, but none surfaced."

"They would have been hard to dispose of."

"Yes."

"What about the murder weapon?"

"An onyx bookend, lying near the body."

"Prints?"

"Wiped."

"Pretty cool-headed, for a burglar."

"Sharon, do you mind if we drop the speculation for tonight?" There was an edge to his voice. "I don't usually spend my evenings being grilled about old cases."

"I'm sorry," I said, meaning it.

"That's okay." He reached for the bottle and poured us more wine. "Frankly there's nothing I hate more than a three-year-old open file."

We leaned back in our respective chairs, sipping wine. The embers glowed and crackled. Greg was right: I'd taken unfair advantage of our friendship.

I glanced over at him speculatively. Months ago I'd been wary of bedding down with a cop—a powerful cop, at that. We'd quarreled, made up, quarreled again. Then as I'd come to know him, the reluctance had vanished, only to be replaced by a series of frustrating and almost comical interferences. The last of these, two weeks ago, had been an ill-timed telephone call summoning him to a death scene on Potrero Hill. Entering into an intimate relationship with a homicide lieutenant was no easy feat.

Nor would it be tonight. He had set down his glass and sat relaxed, feet outstretched toward the dying fire, eyes closed. The tired lines were fading from his face.

Well, the man had a right to be exhausted. Tiptoeing, I started to leave him to his hard-earned rest. As I passed, however, he held out his hand and said, "Come sit with me, papoose. The chair's big enough for two."

I slipped onto his lap, close in the circle of his arms, and we kissed as we had many times before. His hand moved to my breast, my waist, and along the curve of my hip. I stiffened, listening.

As if he heard my thoughts, Greg raised his lips from mine. He smiled lazily. "Don't worry, papoose," he said, using the nickname I was beginning to tolerate. "Before you got here, I turned the phone bell off. Even private eyes and cops deserve some time to devote to one another."

12

I awoke in the tumbled sheets, Greg's arm securely around me. Turning my head, I kissed the crook of his elbow and, when he didn't respond, bit it gently. He chuckled and pulled me against him.

"Again?" I whispered, my lips against his neck.

"Uh-huh, again."

He kissed me, and then his lips traveled down my throat. I pressed him closer, caressing his lean body. We went slowly, all gentle action and reaction, then more insistently.

At one point, as he moved above me, I opened my eyes and saw his face, tensed and flushed with pleasure. And just then, before all thought became fragmented, I reflected how good it was to be able to give and receive. . . .

We lay beside each other for a while, hands touching, quiet. Then I moved up on one elbow to say something and, in the motion, glimpsed the orange numbers of the digital clock on the nightstand.

"Good lord!" I exclaimed, sitting up.

Greg frowned and smoothed back his rumpled blond hair. "I'm not *that* bad a sight in the morning, am I?"

"It's quarter to ten!" I hopped out of bed.

He raised himself up on one elbow, appreciative eyes moving over my body. "So?"

"I'm late!" I headed for the shower. "I don't suppose you happen to have a shower cap?"

"Jesus Christ! Sleeping with a private eye is as bad as screwing another cop!" he exclaimed. "Second drawer on the right. There's also a fresh toothbrush and paste."

I located the cap and got into the shower, rankled at the availability of these conveniences. The extra pillow he'd charmingly produced from the closet last night took on unpleasant overtones. Just how many women used that pillow anyway? And what was this about screwing another cop?

Well, hell, I'd worry about that later. The lieutenant was a fine bed partner and, in the course of the night, he'd expressed similar sentiments about me. Now it was time to show him I was also a fine private eye. Toward that end, I must get to Prince Albert's Lighthouse before noon.

This time I drove directly down Natoma Street and parked on the sidewalk, as the residents did. The place had a sleepy, Sunday morning feeling, and the only person in evidence was Prince Albert himself, who rushed from his shop as I approached. His ginger hair stuck out wildly from under his top hat, and the tails of his gray velvet frock coat billowed. He carried a cardboard carton.

"Hello," I called. "I've come to learn the tricks of your trade."

He stopped midway on the sidewalk and almost dropped the carton. His puckish face was blank for a moment, and then recognition flowed across it. "Damn!" he exclaimed. "I'd clean forgotten about you."

"After you went and lost my clue?"

He set the carton next to a blue panel truck and opened its rear door. "I don't mean I had forgotten you, only our appointment. And now I'm late."

I glanced at my watch. It was only eleven. "Late for what?"

He gestured distractedly. "There's been a problem out at the show. One of my supporting beams broke and destroyed some fixtures. I have to replace them."

"That's too bad! Were they valuable?"

"In terms of the time I'd put into them, yes. Each fixture is hand-crafted. I'm not one of the big operators like Victoriana, you see; with me it's an art, a labor of love. I sell a few fixtures a month, live over the shop, frugally." He took off his top hat and smoothed his hair, replacing the red-plumed creation carefully. "You can understand why I'm upset. And why I must break our appointment."

Disappointed, I nodded. "Can we make it another time?"

"Sure." He fished in the pocket of his frock coat and produced a card. "Give me a call. Once the show is over, I'm all yours." He slammed the door of the truck, ran around to the driver's side, and was gone in a cloud of exhaust.

Reflexively I noted the license number of the truck and jotted it on the card. Yes, his distress seemed genuine, but, no, I didn't trust Prince Albert.

Now what? I had hours to kill before Eleanor van Dyne's house tour. All Souls and Hank were a likely alternative. I rumbled down the narrow street in the MG and turned toward the Bernal Heights district.

The big brown Victorian—Italianate, I now knew—stood on a sloping street across from a triangular park. I wedged my car between two that illegally extended around the corner, thus imparting an aura of respectability to both. Although it was Sunday, Hank would be here. He, along with several other associates, occupied free rooms on the second story that were the cooperative's way of compensating for dismally low salaries.

At the rear of the first floor was a big nineteen-fifties-style kitchen. A couple of attorneys sat at the round table near the window, eating breakfast with the company of the Sunday paper. When I asked for Hank, one of them muttered, "Law library."

Unlike Wintringham's Victorians, the rooms of this one had been divided and partitioned until they provided no hint of the classical floor plan. My own office, in fact, was little more than a converted closet. I went back down the hall and entered a door on the right.

Hank sat at the table beside a sign that read, "Please return books to shelves when you're finished." A pile of *California Appellate Reports* and *Deering's California Codes* attested to its effectiveness. Hank looked up when I came in, his eyes tired behind thick horn-rimmed glasses.

I sat across the table from him. "How you doing?"

"Fair."

"Only fair?"

"It's been a rough weekend."

I remembered: He'd had to break the news to Jake's family. "How did it go with Mrs. Kaufmann?"

"Not bad, considering." He took off his glasses and polished them on the tail of his plaid flannel shirt. "She's a real gutsy lady."

"That's what one of Jake's employees said. I understand she intends to keep on running the business."

Hank replaced his glasses. "We didn't go into it. If she does, I guess my services will be required."

"Hank," I said, leaning forward, my hands clasped on the table, "I ought to tell you, we've got a new client."

"David Wintringham, the owner of the house where you found Jake. He called and told me you'd bring his application in. And that you'd agreed to investigate for him. Nice of you to let me know."

I glanced at him to see if he were seriously annoyed. Normally Hank was the most easygoing boss in existence. After a few seconds, I decided he had merely made the remark as an exercise. I said, "I didn't want to bother you on a Saturday."

"Sure." He shut the leatherbound volume in front of him. Hank was a round-the-clock worker, Saturday being no different to him than Tuesday. "So what have you found out?"

Quickly I outlined the events of the last twenty-four hours, omitting only the personal details of my visit to Greg. Hank listened thoughtfully, tapping his forefinger on the edge of the table.

"Nick Dettman," he said when I'd finished.

"He sends his regards."

"Huh."

"He also sent a nice threat to Wintringham through me, which I didn't deliver. And he directly tossed me a threat, which I caught and returned."

Hank's eyes widened. "Dettman did that?"

"Yes. What do you know about him?"

"He was on the Board of Supes for a couple of terms, about five, six years ago." Hank scratched his curly light-brown head. "He didn't do a good job; he's not really able to represent the interests of the black constituency that elected him."

"Why not?"

"He's too middle class. What some people might call an 'oreo.' He got elected on the issues that concern the blacks, but he was only mouthing phrases. The guy just doesn't understand his own people. He sided against them on almost every issue."

"So he wasn't reelected."

"No, not that he didn't try."

"And now?"

"For a while he maintained some power through providing community legal services, but now that the middle class is taking over much of that neighborhood—and the junkies the rest—Dettman's authority is vanishing. If you want an explanation for his threatening you and Wintringham, I'd say it's the reaction of a desperate man."

"He needs power that badly?"

Hank nodded. "He craves it like a junkie. Without it, Nick Dettman is merely another storefront ghetto lawyer."

"So you wouldn't take the threats seriously, then?"

"I didn't say that. Dettman may be an oreo, but he's been on Haight Street a long time, and he has contacts with some rough characters. Take his threats very seriously. Watch it, Shar. I mean it."

The gravity of his tone sent a shiver along my spine. "Don't worry. I will." My watch read noon: time to grab some lunch and change my clothes for the house tour. I stood up.

"Oh, Shar." Hank's tone was elaborately casual. "You didn't finish with your story."

Instantly I knew what was coming. "Yes, I did."

"Nope." A teasing light appeared in his eyes. "How'd it go with the lieutenant?"

"I told you, he didn't like the idea of my investigating the case, but he couldn't—"

"You know what I mean." Hank had introduced Greg and me, and took what I considered an unnatural interest in the progress of our relationship.

I backed toward the door. "He also gave me the results of the postmortem, and . . ."

"Come on, Shar."

I stepped into the hall, feeling smug. "I'll see you later."

Hank called, "Other women have said he's very good."

I whirled, glaring. There it was again: other women.

"Is he?" Hank persisted.

Irritated at my flash of jealousy, I spat out, "Yes! And if you want the whole story, why don't you ask him how good *I* am!" Then, mortified, I clapped my hand to my mouth and fled down the hall, Hank's goddamned chuckles following me.

13

Rosettes. Pilasters. Colonettes. Cornices. Witch's caps. Gables. Finials.

By six o'clock my feet hurt and my mind was crammed with more architectural details than I'd ever hoped to possess. I knew that the usual San Francisco lot was twenty-five by one hundred feet; that most Victorians shared the same long narrow floor plan; that they were constructed from California's then-abundant redwood trees.

The wood in the dining room of the Haas-Lilienthal House, where I now stood, was golden oak, however. So Eleanor van Dyne informed me as I reached for my seventh cheese-and-cracker. When I'd gone home to change into the conservative black pantsuit appropriate for this occasion, I'd neglected to eat and now, as well as being footsore, I was starving.

As politely as possible with a mouthful of Danish tilsit and Ritz cracker, I murmured my appreciation of the highly polished wainscoting. Van Dyne had taken a liking to me, presumably because I'd claimed to share her views on color. I wanted to keep her talking.

I asked, "How come Salvation Incorporated is holding this reception at Heritage's headquarters?" The mansion, an impressive combination of Queen Anne and Stick styles, had been donated to that foundation by the heirs of the original owners some years before. It was open for public tours and private parties such as this, but it seemed odd that van Dyne's group would hold their wine-and-cheese tasting here when they had a perfectly good mansion of their own.

Van Dyne helped herself to another glass of wine from the sideboard. She had a surprising capacity. "Our headquarters on California Street is currently undergoing redecoration and, as usual, it's behind schedule. When it became apparent it wouldn't be ready for our tour, Heritage very generously offered to let us hold the reception here. We are not rivals; we're all in the preservation effort together."

I glanced around at the crowd, most of whom were middle-aged and appeared well heeled. "How did you get into this line of work?" I asked. "Preservation, I mean."

"I'm a fifth-generation San Franciscan. My family had a mansion far more splendid than this one, on Van Ness Avenue. Unfortunately it was dynamited following the 'quake in oh-six."

As Nick Dettman had mentioned last night, Van Ness, the widest street in the city, had been used as a firebreak. The Army Engineers had dynamited all the buildings on the east side of it to stop the spread of the flames that were the real cause of the postearthquake destruction.

Van Dyne went on, "At any rate, my family has always had a sense of civic duty. Others of my means," she added contemptuously, "may prefer to spend their days at I. Magnin fashion shows, but I feel it's important to make a contribution if you have the leisure to do so."

I knew which people she spoke of: They were the ones who went to the opening night of the opera season expressly to show off their designer gowns. To bring the subject closer to my investigation, I said, "Your motivation makes me think of David Wintringham. I believe it was a family mansion that interested him in the preservationist effort."

The lines around van Dyne's mouth hardened. "The resemblance stops there."

"I don't understand. Aren't the Wintringhams another old San Francisco family?"

She raised her eyebrows, as if this were the first time it had occurred to her. "Yes, they are. Fourth generation. It's hard to understand how. . . . Of course, David's great-grandmother was only a Schuyler. Perhaps that explains it." She seemed to be talking more to herself than to me.

"Explains what?"

She made a quick gesture of dismissal. "Never mind. You

wouldn't understand. How long have you lived in San Francisco, dear?"

"About nine years, both here and in Berkeley. I'm originally from San Diego."

"Not long enough. Not nearly long enough."

The words stung. I considered myself a stable resident of the city. I certainly knew it better than most people. I had a job, I voted, I even planned to buy a house or a condominium someday. Who was van Dyne, to intimate I didn't belong? Swallowing my annoyance, I said, "But you say you differ from David Wintringham. How so?"

"Let's start with the father, Richard. He may have been fond of the family home, but at the same time he created those stucco monstrosities out in the Avenues. And do you know what he did to those other houses in the Steiner Street block?"

I shook my head.

"He carved them up into apartments. Stripped them of their original fixtures. Walled up fireplaces when he didn't just plain rip them out."

I recalled the living room of the house where I'd first met Wintringham and Charmaine. "David is restoring them to the original, though."

"So he says. If he does, he's got his work cut out for him. The worst of it is the exteriors. They've either been covered with asbestos siding or stuccoed over, all in the interest of postwar modernity, to say nothing of saving on paint."

"What will he have to do, remove the stucco and asbestos?"

"Yes. It's a painstaking process. If he's lucky, there will be scars on the wood beneath that will show where the original ornamentation was and what it was like. A good woodworker can match up old pieces of trim with the scars or, if it's unavailable, mill new ones. But, if I know David, he'll just toss on whatever he thinks looks good, paint it garishly, and sell it to the highest bidder."

"I take it your organization doesn't—"

"Let me tell you about Salvation Incorporated. We advocate

exact restoration, down to every detail, strictly as the homes were when they were built. Unfortunately, David doesn't have the patience for that. And the worst of his crimes is his use of color."

"You mean exterior?"

"Interior, too. The decor. . . . But don't get me started on that."

Van Dyne's voice had become shrill. To calm her, I said, "I agree with you about the color."

"So you mentioned." She modulated her tone. "Gray was the preferred exterior color in San Francisco's Victorian era, and the restorations should reflect that. Sometimes white was used. The trim was glossy black. Vestibules were painted to simulate mahogany."

"A lot of things in the Victorian homes seem to have been imitations," I commented, recalling fake balconies, simulated leather wallpapers, and painted-on wood grain from the tour.

"Yes, the Victorians prized the art of imitation, in spite of the real materials being available, often at far less cost. Victorians loved nothing more than for things to seem exactly the opposite of what they were."

"It sounds hypocritical."

"Admittedly it was a hypocritical age. But that was the way it was, and the restorations should adhere to the tradition. These multicolored abominations only came into vogue in the nineteen sixties."

"By abominations, you include what Jake Kaufmann created?"

"Please do not dignify his work with the word 'created'!" Van Dyne spoke through her teeth.

"You disliked Jake?"

"Personally, no. In fact, I rather liked him."

"Is that why you dropped your suit?"

She patted her gray-blond coif, eyes evasive. "That, and other factors."

"Such as?"

She glanced around as if she were afraid someone might

overhear us. "Expense, of course. It would, of course, have gone to the state supreme court. They all do. Merely to have the briefs printed costs a small fortune. And, of course, I liked Jake enough not to want to ruin him financially . . ." She stopped, a clock that had run down.

Of course. I looked sharply at van Dyne, and she turned to the sideboard for another glass of wine, even though the one she held was half full. There had to be some other reason for dropping the suit, one she didn't want to talk about. Expense, to van Dyne and her financier husband, would have meant very little once her fury was aroused, and I sensed her capacity for fury was extensive. What, I wondered, could this fashionable crusader have to hide?

She turned back to me, her confusion banished.

I asked, "Who do you think killed Jake?"

The question didn't startle her. Probably there had been plenty of speculation in preservationist circles. "I don't know. Certainly none of us would kill a person for using the wrong combination of paints."

I hadn't implied it was one of them, but that must have been on all their minds. "Most likely it wasn't anyone who was intimate with the process of restoration," I said.

"Oh? Why?"

I described the conditions in which I had found the body. "Whoever tried to fake that accident did a poor job," I concluded. "A person who knew about painting and plastering would not have made those mistakes."

Van Dyne nodded thoughtfully. "Yes, I see. That lets out quite a few people."

"It certainly lets out David Wintringham. And Charmaine."

"It lets out anyone who has been around those houses enough to pay attention to how the work is done. The Italianate where David and his friend live was fully restored over two years ago. Any of them would have had ample opportunity to observe."

She was right; it eliminated French and Paul Collins, too.

Prince Albert? How much would a fixture manufacturer know about painting? Dettman or Hart or angry blacks from the ghetto streets? Their ignorance was even more likely.

Van Dyne looked toward the dining room door. I followed her gaze. There, by the red-marble fireplace in the second parlor, stood Prince Albert. He was beckoning to van Dyne, but when he saw me he whirled toward the hall.

"Excuse me," van Dyne said, "someone I must speak with." She hurried through the crowd after him.

Thoughtfully, I sipped my wine. What was Prince Albert doing here? Why wasn't he at the home show? And what was his connection with van Dyne? Naturally all the preservationists would know one another, but those two seemed a strange pair. I threaded my way through the second parlor and looked into the hall. Van Dyne and Prince Albert were nowhere in sight. Probably she'd taken him into some area of the house off limits to outsiders.

Well, I couldn't follow them there, but I could locate Prince Albert's panel truck and see where he would go next. I set my wineglass on a passing tray and left.

The truck was parked only two blocks away. If I hurried, I could fetch my car and idle up the street until my quarry returned. But then again. . . . I slipped behind the truck and tested the rear doors.

Yes, Prince Albert hadn't locked them. In fact, the lock was broken. I glanced over my shoulder. Although dusk had fallen, this was a well-traveled street and the buildings on it had many windows. Suppose someone had seen Prince Albert park the truck and now saw a strange woman climb in? Would he call the police or simply mind his own business, as so many did in this age of noninvolvement? I'd have to take the chance.

I climbed into the back of the truck, conscious of headlights from passing cars. Three cardboard cartons rested there, including the one I thought I'd seen Prince Albert load earlier. Had he really gone to the trade show to replace his broken fixtures? Or had he merely made up that story to avoid talking to me?

I crawled forward, wishing it were not necessary to keep my back to the doors. As I reached for the first box my ears strained for an approaching footfall. I grasped the lid and lifted it. Stared down inside. My lips parted at what I saw.

A shade. Tiffany, it must be. Leaves, tiny pieces of glass in red, gold, and brown. A broad grin of teeth. And the eye, greenish yellow. The Cheshire Cat's Eye.

Voices sounded on the sidewalk, and I began to tremble, all senses alert for danger. The voices passed. Controlling myself, I crept further forward and opened the other two boxes. More leaves. Two more grins. Two more eyes.

Replicas, naturally. Prince Albert must have cast these off the original. Gingerly, I lifted the lamp. Yes, the tubular piece of metal I had found at the murder scene was a delicate bronze tree limb that held a bulb. But where had the broken lamp gone? It wasn't the original; it was electric. So was this one. Was the original in one of the other boxes?

Footsteps on the sidewalk made me almost drop the lamp. I replaced it in the carton and flattened against the wall of the truck. I held my breath, torn between hiding and taking flight.

The footsteps, like the voices before, passed. I scrambled toward the rear doors, slamming them shut behind me as I jumped from the truck.

14

I idled at the curb in my MG. Its engine coughed, reminding me of its long-needed tune-up. Well, I'd take care of that later, after I'd unraveled the puzzle of the Cheshire Cat's Eye.

Traffic streamed past me. I was on Franklin Street, a one-way artery to the Golden Gate Bridge and Marin County. At least it would not be easy for Prince Albert to spot me among the other cars.

I tensed as I saw his wiry figure lope down the steps of the Haas-Lilienthal mansion and head toward his truck. As soon as I'd fled, I was sorry I hadn't had the nerve to stay and examine the other two cartons, but now I felt a flood of relief. Had I, Prince Albert would surely have discovered me.

The truck pulled out into a break in traffic. So did I.

The truck stayed in the left-hand lane. I kept two cars between us. Just when I had decided Prince Albert was headed for Lombard Street and perhaps the bridge, he veered to the curb. I screeched into a driveway up the block.

The truck's headlights illuminated a debris box, one of the open-topped truck trailers that were a familiar sight in front of buildings being renovated. In this case, the house was an ugly pink stucco-and-brick structure that needed all the help it could get. Prince Albert went to the back of the truck and removed one of the cardboard cartons.

Expecting him to go into the house, I peered through my side window, trying to get its number. Instead, he approached the dumpster. With a lob that would have done an NBA player credit, he heaved the carton in, then ran back to his truck and jumped into the driver's seat.

I backed out of the driveway, let a passing car slide between the truck and me, and continued the chase. Prince Albert's vehicle turned left and meandered into the depths of Pacific Heights. I realized he was looking for another debris box; possibly he felt the lamps might be traced if he disposed of them all together. He had picked a good area to do this: With the number of restorations and condominium conversions going on in this affluent neighborhood, the dumpster population was high.

Sure enough, Prince Albert found another box and repeated his maneuver. He then turned down a side street, drove a block, and, in front of a large apartment house, disposed of the last carton. I noted the location of each dumpster and continued following the truck.

Soon it became apparent that Prince Albert was headed home, his night's work done. To make sure, I followed him as far as where Natoma Street branched off Sixth, then turned back toward the last dumpster to collect my evidence. I left the MG idling and ran up to the debris box, peering on tiptoe over its side.

The carton was gone. I stared in amazement.

The city was divided between those who dumped into the debris boxes and those who scavenged from them. I had once seen a bicycle with only one wheel disappear within three minutes of being tossed in, but this was still fast work. Whoever had gotten here before me must have been delighted with his find. I ran back to the car and U-turned. The box in front of the ugly house on Franklin would be my next stop.

Again I left the car idling at the curb. As I passed the house, I glanced up. It was three stories, and its curving tower windows were dark. With a mental start, I realized it was a Queen Anne whose facade had been covered with stucco and bricks. Eleanor van Dyne would have died on the spot. I surveyed the house carefully. Not a light showed. Probably it was vacant for the restoration.

This dumpster was piled higher than the other one. Most of the debris was wood, plaster, and assorted junk, but I spotted Prince Albert's carton on top of the heap. Straining, I reached for it. My hands fell short by several feet.

I sighed and looked up and down the street. Thank God there were no pedestrians! People in cars wouldn't notice me climbing up on the dumpster or, if they did, wouldn't care. But a person on foot might wonder why a young woman in a tailored black pantsuit was scaling a heap of trash.

The sides of the box were indented in places, providing frequent, if slippery, toeholds. I pulled myself up and bent forward over the top, stretching my five-foot-six frame to its full extent. My fingers missed the box and encountered something slimy. I yanked my hands back and carefully hoisted myself closer. My nostrils flared at the unmistakable odor of rotting cabbage. Someone had tossed his garbage in here.

My nose still wrinkled, I pulled myself higher and once

more reached for the carton. I grabbed its top and pulled. It resisted, and I teetered precariously. Oh, God, I thought, don't let me fall into that slime!

Regaining my balance, I pulled again, and the box moved toward me. I almost dropped it hauling it over the side, but soon it was safe on the ground beside me. I dragged it back, into the shelter of a brick archway that led to the alley at the side of the ugly pink house, and shined my pencil flash on the contents. The rich colors of stained glass gleamed. It was one of the lamps, all right, but in the darkness I couldn't tell if it was electric or kerosene.

I was so busy reaching for my find that I didn't take note of my surroundings. By the time I became aware of the footsteps behind me, a dark figure loomed up. It slammed me into the side of the archway. I cried out as my cheek scraped against the bricks, and a hand clamped over my mouth. An arm circled me, and my attacker began to drag me into the alley.

I tried to wrench free. I tried to get into one of the holds I'd learned in self-defense class. Nothing worked. He—was it a he?—dragged me farther.

I was dimly aware of a fire escape and trash chutes above. Broken glass crunched underfoot. We careened past a can under one of the chutes and slammed into a fence at the other side. It almost gave way under our combined weights. There we rested. My attacker's breath was harsh in my ear. He spoke.

"Now you listen, bitch." The words were thick with the accent of the black ghetto. "You gonna get out of the Western Addition, you hear? You gonna stay away from that Wintringham and forget about everything. Or else you gonna get blown away."

The words chilled me. I tried to calm myself. This was merely a threat. He did not intend to kill me now.

"You got it, bitch?" His lips were still close to my ear.

I tried to shake my head yes, but his hand clamped too tightly across my mouth.

"I said, you got it?"

I made a strangled sound.

Apparently he took it as an affirmative, because next I was careening farther back into the alley, stumbling to avoid a fall, pitching along at tremendous speed from his shove. I grabbed at the wall of the house, missed, and ended up in a heap on the cold pavement. My attacker's footsteps thundered down the passageway. Before I could pull myself up, he was gone.

I sank back onto the ground, breathing hard from both exertion and terror. A threat, I told myself, only a threat. You've had those before. And you're not hurt, not really.

A black man. Dettman? No, Dettman was paunchy and soft. This man had been lean and strong. Johnny Hart? No, not tall enough. Who? A stranger. Someone Dettman or Hart had hired to do his dirty work.

And how had he found me, anyway? I'd been on a house tour, chased Prince Albert all over, and visited two dumpsters. I shivered, realizing he could have been following me the whole time, awaiting his chance.

A rustling sound down by the garbage cans brought me back to the present.

Oh, my God, rats! San Francisco had a rat problem. Its alleys were full of them.

I jumped to my feet and rushed toward the street.

When I reached the brick archway, I remembered the cardboard carton I'd rescued from the dumpster. Frantically I searched for it. All I found was my pencil flash. The carton had vanished along with my attacker.

I stood, rumpled and dumbfounded on the sidewalk. The threat I could understand; Hank had warned me to take Dettman and his playmates seriously. And, in spite of his helpfulness, I still had my doubts about Johnny Hart.

But this—why? What on earth could either of them want with the Cheshire Cat's Eye?

15

The rain had begun in the early morning hours, but it wasn't the only thing dampening my spirits. I sat cross-legged on my bed, warming my hands on a cup of coffee. The night before I had conquered my fears and searched the third dumpster for the remaining lamp. It, too, was gone. All I had to show for my efforts were bruises and a couple of painful scrapes from the struggle in the alley of the house on Franklin Street.

"What the hell did the Cheshire Cat look like anyway?" I muttered. It had been many years since I'd read *Alice in Wonderland*.

I went to the bookcase that covered one wall of my studio apartment and rummaged through the children's books. I'd saved them from my mother's most recent spring-cleaning fit, which had extended dangerously to the attic of the rambling old house in San Diego. Above the swish of her broom, I'd pleaded with her to save them for me.

No, they were cluttering up the attic and had to go.

Well, at least let the grandkids have them, then.

No way. They had plenty of their own books.

Well, what about my own kids? I might have kids someday.

At this point, my mother had directed a stern gaze at me that said she'd believe it the day I sprouted wings and flew. After all, I wasn't getting any younger, was I? No, if I wanted to save the books I could darn well lug them to San Francisco.

Ergo, children's books next to my old sociology texts.

I pulled out an illustrated copy of *Alice* and thumbed through it, pausing to smile over the picture of the hookah-smoking caterpillar. Toward the middle, I found Alice staring up at a grinning cat in a tree.

"Would you tell me, please, which way I ought to go from here?"

"That depends a good deal on where you want to go," said the Cat.

"I don't much care where—" said Alice.

"Then it doesn't matter which way you go," said the Cat.

"—so long as I get *somewhere*," Alice added as an explanation.

"Oh, you're sure to do that," said the Cat, "if you only walk long enough."

I sighed and shut the book. Life imitating art, perhaps? I was sure to get someplace myself, if I thought long enough. But wasn't there a shortcut? Didn't Charmaine work with stained glass?

I went to the phone and dialed Wintringham's residence. Paul Collins answered. David was on the job site. Could he help me instead?

"Yes. Do you have Charmaine's number?"

There was a pause. "Are you making any headway with the murder investigation?"

"Some."

"Well, that's good."

"Now, about Charmaine."

"She's got a house on Buena Vista Heights. The number's in the book, under 'C.' She's listed like she lives—single-namedly." Collins wished me luck and hung up.

I drained my coffee cup and headed for the shower.

Charmaine lived in a brown-shingled bungalow on the east side of Buena Vista Park, high above the Haight-Ashbury. I followed a brick path alongside the house, as the decorator had instructed me over the phone. Tall, spike-leaved palms dripped water as I made my way down the slippery slope toward the basement door.

Today Charmaine was not her usual fashionable self. She wore faded jeans and a baggy sweater with a rip in one elbow, and the polish on her red talons was chipped. Even in her dishabille, however, she wore fresh makeup and a chic turban over her hair. She admitted me cheerfully and led the way past washtubs and storage bins to what she called her workroom. It contained two large tables made of sawhorses and plywood, and its walls were honeycombed with racks that held pieces of colored glass.

"Have a seat." She waved her hand at a stool next to one of the tables. "You caught me at a good time. This is real shit work, and I need company." She picked up a stiff-bristled brush and began rubbing at the table. It was covered with what looked like dirty snow, beneath which I could make out a pattern of glass and metal.

"What are you working on?"

"A window." She brushed some of the powder aside. "It's for a lawyer's office."

The window depicted the scales of justice in blues and golds and reds.

"Nice," I said. "My boss would go crazy over that."

"Send him around. This is almost done, and I could use another commission. But don't tell him I can produce one fast; this took four years, working in my spare time."

"Four years!"

"I make my living from decorating. It leaves very little time for hobbies. And I have other stained-glass projects, too."

I watched her hands as she brushed the powder. "What does that do?"

"I just puttied around the lead strips. This stuff is called whiting; it picks up the oil in the putty and tones down the lead, makes it look older."

"Is it hard work?"

"Boring. And messy. If you weren't here to talk to, I'd wear my surgical mask to keep from breathing the powder into my lungs."

"Listen, if it's dangerous, go ahead."

"No, it's not that bad. And I really don't like to wear the mask." She paused, looking at me. "On the phone you said you need information."

"Yes, about glass."

"You've come to the right place. What?"

"Do you know anything about Tiffany lamps?"

Charmaine's brush slowed, then picked up its vigorous tempo. "A fair amount. I've read a few books on the subject."

"As a layman, how would you go about telling a real Tiffany from a fake?"

"Easy. I'd look for the signature on the base. Tiffany Studios always signed them."

Unfortunately I hadn't seen any of the bases of Prince Albert's lamps.

"What about the glass? Could you tell from that?"

"The quality of the glass would at least place it in time."

"How so?"

She set down the brush and went to one of the wall racks. Pulling out a piece of red glass, she held it up to the light. "Look at this."

"It's pretty."

She set it on the rack and reached into a higher one. "But now, look at this."

Again, it was red glass, but it shone as if with an inner light. I sucked in my breath. "Lovely."

Charmaine nodded. "The second is old—I got it from one of the houses David remodeled. The first is a contemporary American product. Glass is getting worse, more like plastic all the time."

"It must be, if even I can tell." And indeed I could. The second sample seemed more like what I had seen last night in the beam of my pencil flash. Or was that merely wishful thinking?

Charmaine replaced the glass and took up her brush again. "So why do you need to know about Tiffany? Is it part of the work you're doing for David? What kind of work is it, by the way?"

I was surprised he hadn't told her. "I'm investigating Jake Kaufmann's murder—and, as a result of that, David's father's."

This time the brush stopped. "Why?"

"They seem to be related. Listen, can I describe a lamp shade for you? Maybe you can tell me something about it." A growing suspicion forced me on.

Charmaine nodded, her eyes on the dirty snow.

I told her about the Cheshire Cat's Eye: the leaves, the teeth, the gleaming yellow-green stone.

"Where did you see that?" she demanded.

"I can't say right now. Could it be a Tiffany?"

She wet her lips. "Does this have something to do with Jake's murder?"

I ignored her question. "You've seen a lamp like that before, haven't you?"

She bent her head. The brush forced the dirty snow into intricate patterns. "It could be a Tiffany. The motif of autumn leaves was common with Tiffany Studios' products. Lamps with tree trunks for bases and leaves for shades were typical. You say this shade had an irregularly shaped upper and lower border?"

I nodded. "That's right."

"It's one of the more complex designs." She kept her head bent over the table.

"What about the eye?"

As if she felt it stare at her, she looked up. "What about it?"

"Is that typical of Tiffany?"

Pausing, she considered. "He did a lot with peacocks' eyes. Yes, I guess it could be said to be typical."

I pressed on. "What about the teeth?"

"Well, Tiffany perfected iridescent glass. But, no, I never saw one of his trees with teeth sticking out." She tried to smile, but it came off false. "If the lamp is a Tiffany, it would have to have been specially commissioned."

I could bet she knew by whom. "The eye—what would it be?"

"Glass, made to resemble a jewel." She answered too fast.

"Did Tiffany ever use real jewels, semiprecious stones, perhaps?"

"Not that I know of."

"But could he have?"

With an agitated motion, Charmaine dropped the brush and began to pace, her arms folded across her breasts. "He could have. They would fit in, just like the glass jewels did. But I don't understand, Sharon."

"Neither do I."

She stopped, a foot away from me. "What?"

"There's something I don't understand, too. Why does the lamp I just described have you so frightened?"

She took a step backward.

"What is it with this lamp, Charmaine?"

She folded her arms tighter.

"Are you afraid because you copied the shade for Prince Albert?"

She was silent.

"Were the shades the other stained-glass projects that slowed your progress on this window?"

Strength seemed to leave her, and she sagged against the table. "You knew that all along, didn't you?"

I hadn't, but . . . "Did Prince Albert commission them?"

She bit her lip. "Yes," she finally said, "three of them. He had the original for me to work from. He *claimed* he'd gotten it in a junk shop."

Reacting to the stressed word, I said, "But you didn't believe him."

"No one would sell a real Tiffany to a junk shop. And no junk dealer would let it go for what Al could afford."

I'd had some experience with junk shops, however. It was possible for real treasure to go unnoticed among the trash. Or maybe Prince Albert had thought it worth more than what Charmaine assumed he could afford. I regarded her thoughtfully.

"Anyway," she added, "I found out later that Larry . . ."

"What about Larry?"

She snatched off her stylish turban and shook out her bell-like hair. "Forget it."

"Charmaine, you brought it up."

"No, forget it."

"I can't."

"Oh, God." She wiped her brow with the turban. "This *does* have to do with Jake's murder, and Larry will get in trouble."

I didn't answer.

"If I tell you, he'll kill me." She paused, startled at the implication of what she'd just said.

"What about Larry, Charmaine?"

She took a deep breath. "Okay. Okay. When I started working on the shades for Al, I showed the lamp to Larry. I couldn't believe it—that Al had found a real Tiffany in a junk shop."

"What was Larry's reaction?"

"At first he was cool. He asked what it was worth. But then when I told him, he got furious. He said if he'd known that, he never would have let it out of his hands."

I felt a flash of excitement. "When did he have it?"

She shook her head, hair swinging. "He wouldn't say. He told me to forget he'd mentioned it. I shouldn't have told you."

I couldn't respond to her woebegone expression, so great was my excitement. So Larry French had once possessed the Cheshire Cat's Eye. That could make him a murderer—or someone who knew who the murderer was. "Charmaine, what's the story with you and Larry?"

"Story?"

"He doesn't treat you very well. Why do you put up with him?"

Her gaze slipped away from mine. "Larry's all right. He puts on a tough front for other people but, really, he's quite decent. And he has contacts. He's promised me some very lucrative design work for important people in Hollywood. If I can break in there I'd have it made. And I will. I've got what it takes." It sounded like a lesson she'd learned by rote and now repeated with declining conviction.

"That's right," I said. "Larry used to be in show business."

Charmaine nodded. "He put on all the big concerts. He knew all the stars. All I need is to decorate one big star's house and I'll be on my way."

"Why's Larry no longer in show business?"

"You don't know?" Charmaine's wide eyes swung to mine.

"No."

"God. I thought everyone did. At one of the concerts he put on—his last—there was a disturbance. Nothing like what happened at Altamont, but people started slugging it out. Larry got into the fray and, well . . ."

"And what?"

"Well, he killed a man. It was ruled self-defense, but he *did* kill him, and after that no one would touch a Larry French production with a ten-foot pole."

16

The Cheshire Cat's Eye: Larry French had once possessed it; with Charmaine's help, Prince Albert had copied it; and, last night, my unknown assailant had seized it. Were these people linked together only by their interest in a Tiffany lamp? Or was there a stronger connection? Determining that would involve a risk, given the warning I'd received, but it was one I'd have to take.

The weather served to minimize my danger. I took a floppy-brimmed rainhat from the back of the MG and pinned my hair high on my head before I stuffed the hat over it. If my attacker was on the lookout for a woman with long black hair, he wouldn't see her.

I parked on Steiner Street, across from Wintringham's houses, and hesitated, contemplating the locked glove compartment. Finally I took out the .38 Chief's Special that rested there, loaded it, and slipped it into the outer compartment of my shoulder bag. I approached Johnny Hart's Kansas City Barbecue from the rear.

The proprietor was in the kitchen, lighting the gas fires under the big vats of sauce. He frowned, not recognizing me when I came in. I took off the hat and shook out my hair.

"Oh, it's you." He turned back to his sauce pots. "That a disguise or something?"

"Yep, it's all part of being a private eye." I studied the set of his shoulders, the steadiness of his hands.

"Huh." Hart flicked a drop of water into the deep-fat fryer. It popped and crackled. He didn't look or sound like a man who had been surprised by someone whom he'd hired a thug to rough up.

I sat down at the chopping block, feeling suddenly queasy from tension and the smell of stale grease.

Hart glanced at me. "You all right?"

"I'll be fine."

"Can I get you something to speed up this fineness?" His words were mocking, but he flashed a yellow-toothed smile.

"Do you have any milk?"

"One milk coming up." He turned to the stainless-steel refrigerator. "Big, tough private eyes always drink milk?"

"Only when they can't get Kool-aid."

Hart set a glass in front of me, and I drank half of it quickly. My queasiness subsided, and I sipped the rest.

"Now," Hart said in a low voice, drawing up a chair, "let's cut the smart talk and get down to business. Why're you here?"

The wary currents of racial distrust stirred once more. I sensed Hart didn't want to like me because I was white and excused it by reminding himself of my Indian ancestry. Unfortunately, I was too middle class for the excuse to have much validity.

"I'm here because I need more information."

"I gave you enough of that on Saturday."

"It was enough then, not now."

"Girl, I ain't got no more to give you."

"Not even about who you hired to rough me up?"

Hart's face was impassive, but he leaned back in his chair and regarded me silently for a minute. "You dreaming, girl."

"Am I? Let me tell you about my adventure last night." I recounted my struggle in the alley.

When I had finished, Hart stroked his chin thoughtfully.

"So because this person was black, you think I was behind it."

"You. Or Dettman."

Hart looked genuinely offended. "I don't beat up on women or tell anybody else to do it for me."

"Then that leaves Nick."

Hart sighed, staring off beyond me. "All right, but don't you ever let on that I was the one told you. There's a dude in the neighborhood name of Raymond, only everybody calls him Raymond-the-Hit-Man."

"Hit man!" My voice rose.

"Hush." Hart held up a cautioning hand. "Raymond don't hit much; when he tries he usually misses. But he does fix things. You know, you want a debt collected, call Raymond. You want to even a score, Raymond's your man."

"I get it. So, if Dettman wanted to get me, Raymond's the one he would have used."

"Yeah." Hart looked uncomfortable. "Saturday, when Dettman had me deliver that message to you, he was in here looking for Raymond. Raymond, he's hard to find, don't have no regular address, so when you want him, you pass the word around."

"What does this Raymond look like?"

"He's . . . well, hell, you've seen him."

"When?"

"The night you and your white lawyer friend were here. He's the dude in the leather coat who came in and told me about the murder."

I recalled him, both from then and also from outside Nick Dettman's storefront the next night. "When did Raymond get Dettman's message?"

"I delivered it late Saturday afternoon when he came in for a couple of beers."

So our paths had crossed immediately before Dettman had put out his contract—or whatever you might call it—on me. Dettman had tried to warn me off peaceably, but he already had Raymond lined up as backup. Or had he had more than one job for the "hit man"?

"Is Raymond likely to come after me again?" I asked Hart.

He shrugged. "Depends on how bad Dettman wants to get rid of you."

"Would Raymond actually kill me?"

"Well, he ain't no virgin when it comes to offing people, that's the rumor. But he don't do it for kicks. Dettman would have to pay him plenty."

"Good lord." I stood up, glad of the weight of the gun in my bag. Until I'd exhausted all possible leads, I'd steer clear of Dettman and this part of town.

"Of course," Hart added ruminatively, "like I said, Raymond ain't too good a shot. If you don't get close to him, you shouldn't have any trouble. You got a gun?"

"Yes."

"Keep it handy."

I patted my bag. "Don't worry. What do I owe you for the milk?"

Hart grinned. "Guns and milk. What a way to live. Forget the money; it was worth it to get a look at the private life of a private eye."

"Thanks." I handed him one of my cards. "If you hear any more about Dettman's plans for Raymond, give me a call, will you?"

He glanced at it. "I'll be in touch."

When I peered through the grimy window of Prince Albert's shop, I saw him bent over a piece of machinery at the rear. I stepped inside. Prince Albert looked up, and his face took on a cornered expression. No doubt Charmaine had called to warn him about our conversation.

"What do you want?" he demanded.

"My, my. I thought when the show was over you were going to demonstrate the tricks of your trade for me."

"I'm busy now. I told you to call first."

"Sorry, I forgot. If you don't want to discuss making light fixtures, we can talk about some property you misplaced."

"Misplaced? Misplaced what? Where?"

"You remember the dumpster on Franklin Street, and the one on . . ."

Anger contorting his puckish features, he slammed down the screwdriver he held. I thought how a blow like that could easily crush a man's skull. Or mine, for that matter.

"Look," he said, "I've had enough of your sneaking around and spying on me." He advanced, forcing me back toward the door. "Get out of here."

On the sidewalk, I stood my ground. "I'm out, but this is as far as I'm going."

He looked around in desperation. The only spectator was a child riding a tricycle down the middle of the wet street.

"All right!" Prince Albert exclaimed, slamming the door of the shop. "Then *I'll* go!" He strode down the sidewalk toward Sixth Street.

I tagged along in his footsteps. "One of the lamps you threw into the dumpsters had to be the original. There were three replicas, and one of those got broken when Jake was killed."

Prince Albert turned right on Sixth.

"Part of that replica was my clue, which you dropped in the Bay. I don't suppose you know where the rest of it went."

He went into a corner grocery store.

"When you realized the lamps had something to do with the murder, you went to Eleanor van Dyne. Then you disposed of them. What did she tell you?"

He stopped in front of the refrigerated case and plucked out a six-pack of beer.

"What's van Dyne's role in this?"

At the deli case, he grabbed a salami and some cheese.

"Why'd you go to see her when you should have been at the trade show?"

He flung some money down at the checkout stand and stamped through the door.

"What would van Dyne know about the Cheshire Cat's Eye?"

He turned back toward Natoma Street.

"Why'd you go see her, Prince Albert?"

He turned, waving the salami aloft. "You and your fucking questions! Leave me alone!"

Two children in yellow rain slickers pointed and giggled at the funny man with the sausage. Prince Albert glared at them and then at me.

"Why?" I repeated.

"Oh, Jesus." His voice broke, and it came out almost a sob. "All right. I went to see her because I was afraid."

"Afraid of what?"

We began walking down Natoma Street. "Well, Jesus, there I was reproducing the damned things, displaying them in public! I even had one at the trade show. Do you think I wanted to get mixed up in a murder rap?"

"If you didn't, why did you reproduce the lamp in the first place?"

"Because I didn't know . . ." He stopped under the overhang in front of the shop. Water dripped onto the pavement. "Look, let me start from the beginning. I told you Jake came in here the day he was killed. It was the first time he'd been in for a while, and I showed him the original Tiffany. I thought he'd be impressed at the deal I got, but instead it upset him. He wouldn't say why, but he asked if he could borrow one of the copies. I hated to let it out of my hands, but Jake was a good friend. Anyway, when he turned up dead and you came around with that metal piece, I panicked. I pulled the copy off the floor at the show and the next day I went to ask Eleanor if she'd ever seen or heard of the lamp. I figured it had something to do with the Wintringhams, since Jake was killed in their old house. Because the lamp was so unique, I knew Eleanor would recognize it from a description, if she knew it."

"I take it she did."

"Yes. I believed her; she would know. She told me how it had been stolen when the old man was killed. She got all excited, and I had to swear her to secrecy. I really didn't figure she'd talk about it, though. She has her reasons to stay out of it."

"What reasons?"

Prince Albert shook his head. "Anyway, then I was really panicked. I decided, valuable or not, I had to get rid of the things. And I did, except . . ." He glared accusingly at me.

"Where did you find the original?"

"Junk shop, about six months ago."

It tallied with Charmaine's account, but had the decorator called and briefed him? I'd have to check it out. "Which one?"

"A place down on Salem Street. I was looking for a stove, a goddamned stove, and this lamp turned up instead. The old guy who runs the place didn't know it was valuable, I guess. Or maybe he didn't care. I bought it for a hundred bucks. Now I wish I'd never seen the damned thing."

Salem Street. I knew it well. "What's the name of the store?"

He frowned. "I don't remember. A big old guy runs it. A guy with long gray hair."

"Does he wear army fatigues and a sheepskin jacket?"

"Yeah. You know him?"

"Very well." It was my friend Charlie Cornish. I could count on him to give me the straight story; he kept records of what he bought and sold.

Prince Albert looked eagerly at me. "Then you can check it out. Maybe he'll remember me."

It was not the response of someone who was lying. I studied the lampmaker. In spite of his suspicious behavior, the story had the ring of truth.

"All right," I said, "I'll check. If it's true, good. If not, I'll tell the cops. Don't try to run, because it won't do you any good."

A sheepish smile spread over Prince Albert's face. "Don't worry about me running."

"Why shouldn't I?"

"You've seen my truck. That old heap wouldn't take me across the Bay Bridge."

17

A phone call to Charlie Cornish's junk shop got me a recording. The number had been changed. So he had already moved from Salem Street. The area, once an enclave of secondhand shops, was being razed in the interests of urban renewal. Charlie's new store was on Valencia Street, in the Mission District, not far from my own apartment.

When I arrived, the storefront was bustling with activity. Movers unloaded furniture and crates and hauled them inside. The only thing that reminded me of Charlie's old shop was his scarred oak desk—and Charlie himself, who sat in his swivel chair directing operations. From the back of the store came a shrill barking voice that could only belong to Charlie's new partner, Austin Bigby.

Charlie's eyes brightened when he saw me. "It's about time you paid me a visit!"

I smiled. It had been three months or more since I'd seen the big junkman, but it seemed longer. We'd had daily contact while I was investigating a murder on Salem Street.

Charlie pulled a straight chair out of the jumble and offered it to me. I sat, regarding him fondly. "I guess I'm your first customer."

"Sure are. Can I sell you something?"

"The answers to a few questions."

"Up to your old tricks, huh?"

"Yes."

Charlie was silent for a moment, glowering at a mover who lowered a crate to the floor with a thud. "You still seeing the lieutenant?"

Why did all my male friends have such concern for my love life? "Now and then."

"You don't sound very enthusiastic."

I frowned.

"Sharon, the lieutenant's a good-looking man. You could do worse."

"You sound like my mother."

"You should listen to your mama."

"I do, long distance on the phone every week. Now about those questions . . ."

"Set that down over there," Charlie called to one of the movers. To me, he added, "You really can't get decent help nowadays. They already broke the glass on a jukebox, and Austin's fit to be tied."

"I can hear him."

"Someday he's gonna have a stroke if he keeps it up," Charlie said. "Then I'll be stuck alone with all this junk." He grimaced, but I knew it was only for show. Junk was Charlie's life.

I said, "What I want to ask you is about something of real value."

"I don't know, Sharon." He ran his fingers through his gray mane. "Maybe you better ask Austin; he's the expert."

"This is something you sold on Salem Street, around six months ago. An old lamp with an unusual shade, made to look like a Cheshire Cat hiding in a tree."

Charlie's little eyes narrowed. "Yeah, I remember it. Fellow that bought it was real excited. I knew it was valuable, but what the hell. He really wanted it bad."

Charlie, in spite of appearances, had done well in his business. He could afford an occasional burst of generosity. "What did the guy look like?" I asked.

He grinned. "Weird, but we've got more than our fair share of those in this town. Wore a top hat and a velvet coat. Had floppy ginger hair that kept falling out from under the hat. The only thing that would have improved the get-up was if he'd had a pair of those turned-up shoes with bells on the toes."

I chuckled, imagining Prince Albert's outrage could he hear. "That's my man."

"What'd he do, kill somebody?"

"I doubt it." I really did, now. "Listen, Charlie, in your records is there any way of telling when and from whom you bought that lamp? And if you bought anything else with it?"

"Sure, but finding out will take time; my file cabinet's still on the truck. I can tell you one of the other things I bought with it, though." He rubbed his chin and regarded me slyly. "Sure is a funny coincidence."

"What is?"

"Well, you come in here and ask about that lamp. That's not unusual; you ask a lot of questions. But for you to come in the day after the guy did—"

"What guy?" I exclaimed.

Charlie leaned back in his swivel chair, obviously pleased at surprising me. "Yesterday afternoon, while I was packing all this stuff up, a fellow came into the shop. I told him I was closed, it was Sunday, but he wouldn't listen. Pushy fellow."

"Describe him."

"Short and stocky. Turned-up nose like one of those ugly dogs. Sort of hip. Might have been a rock star—or an accountant trying to look like one."

French. Our paths were crossing.

"Anyway," Charlie went on, "he asked about the lamp, same as you. Then he asked if he could look around. Hell, it was easier to let him wander than to throw him out. Finally he bought this pressed-glass bottle. Because he'd asked about the lamp, it occurred to me that the bottle was one of the things I'd bought with it."

A pressed-glass bottle. Some bottles and flasks had been taken at the time of Richard Wintringham's murder.

"Did you look up who you'd bought it from for him?"

"No. He wasn't interested in that. What he was interested in was the lamp."

That meant he probably knew who had sold the bottle to Charlie. French, in spite of his off-the-wall manner, kept a careful eye on what went on around him. "How long before that file cabinet comes off the truck?"

Charlie glanced at me curiously. "God knows, what with the

way these fellows work. It's important, huh?"

"Very."

"I'll see if I can hurry them up. Why don't you run down the street and pick us up a couple of burritos?"

It was a good way to pass the time. I walked two blocks to a take-out place and stood in line listening to salsa music and stacatto Spanish voices. When I returned with two bean burritos and Cokes, Charlie was on the sidewalk, berating the moving men. They had the filing cabinet halfway out of the truck and looked like they might drop it.

"Come on inside," Charlie told me. "I can't stand to watch."

We went back to his desk and ate our lunch. As we finished the movers struggled in with the cabinet and deposited it near the door.

"Morons," Charlie muttered. "Right where it'll block traffic. I'm not gonna bother them about it, though. I'd rather animal it around myself than watch them operate."

He produced a key ring and opened the cabinet. "Let's see. Six months ago. I didn't have that lamp for long. I'll start eight months back and work forward." He burrowed into the top drawer.

I felt a rush of disappointment. "Are you sure you bought it that recently?"

"No longer than a year."

It didn't fit with the timetable of Richard Wintringham's murder. I hoped Charlie was wrong.

He rustled through the papers for a few minutes, then pulled one out. "Yep. Early October, last fall. The fifth. I bought the lamp, some bottles, and a clock. Clock didn't work, but it sold fast anyway."

"Does it say who you bought them from?"

"Yep."

Excited, I reached for the piece of paper he held. "Who?"

He handed it to me. "Take it easy. You'll have a stroke like Austin's gonna."

I scanned the receipt. The name—Bob Keefer—was unfamiliar, but it was a name, with a phone number and an address. I copied them into my notebook.

Charlie replaced the receipt in his file. "This fellow who sold me the stuff—is he the killer?"

"What makes you think there is one?"

"I know you."

"I see. Do you remember what the man looked like?"

Charlie shook his head. "This business, you get so many people who wander in off the street with stuff. It's like the pawnshop business: one rundown soul after another."

I glanced at his hodgepodge of old stoves and tattered furniture and wondered, as I often had, why Charlie had made dreary objects his life's work. But then, to him, junk was not merely junk, but treasure to be recycled.

The movers were hauling in a refrigerator, and Charlie turned to them. "You bust the freon tube in there, and you've damned well bought you a 'fridge!"

I made for the door, waving good-bye to him. He wouldn't mind my abrupt departure. He knew I'd return eventually with the whole story and a jug of his favorite California mountain red.

18

The address I'd copied from Charlie's receipt was out Mission Street, almost to the Daly City line. It was a bland-looking neighborhood of small stucco homes. I didn't know if they were actually Wintringham row houses, but they fit the bill: eye-like windows and a gaping mouth of a garage beneath. Yes, I decided, if someone had strung chains across those garages, the houses would appear to be undergoing orthodontia.

A pickup truck sat in the driveway of the house I sought. The words "General Contractor" were visible on its door, but the name had been painted out and no new one took its place. I climbed the steps of the house and rang the bell.

A fat woman in stretch pants answered my second ring. She held a cigarette in the corner of her mouth, and ashes dribbled down the front of her overblouse as she said, "Yeah?"

"I'm looking for Bob Keefer. Is he home?"

"You and everybody else. He left around an hour ago. Try Ed's Place."

"Ed's?"

"Bar down on the corner. That's Bob's office." She laughed mirthlessly and stubbed out her cigarette in a planter on the railing.

I got out one of my cards, the kind that merely gave my name and not my profession. "If he comes back before I locate him, will you ask him to give me a call?"

The folds of her fleshy face pulled downward. "Bob in trouble?"

"Not that I know of."

"Is it about a job?"

"Possibly."

"Funny."

"How so?"

"I don't know what the guy who came by earlier wanted, but Bob had that look he gets—kind of foxy, you know—when he smells money. Sure would help. Maybe then he'd pay the back rent on his room and fix that heap so he could get it out of my driveway."

Obviously Prince Albert wasn't the only one with transportation problems. "The contracting business isn't so good?"

"Never is, this time of year. Too much rain, not enough inside work. Still, he should know better, should save up when he's raking in the dough. If he wasn't my own dead sister's boy. . . . But that's another story." She glanced at my card again. "Yeah, I'll have him call you. Jobs are hard to come by."

I thanked her and headed for Ed's.

It was the standard neighborhood bar, with the standard booths and tables and paunchy man behind the bar. A couple of middle-aged women who reminded me of Bob Keefer's aunt sat near the rear. An old man nursed a tall drink and watched a game show on TV. I slipped onto a stool and ordered a beer.

The bartender set it in front of me and took my money, frankly sizing me up. This was the sort of establishment that would draw regulars from the immediate neighborhood and attract very few strangers.

"You know Bob Keefer?" I asked the bartender.

He shrugged.

"His aunt said I might find him here. It's about a job."

The man pursed his lips, then shrugged again. "He could use one. Carpentry business is lousy this time of year."

"Has he been in today?"

"Yeah, about an hour ago. With some guy. They talked, then left together. Don't tell me he's come up with two jobs in one day?"

"Could be."

"Well, if he has, you're out of luck. This guy looked like he could pay."

Did that mean I didn't? "In what way?"

"He looked rich. Denim suit, gold chains, you know the type. They drove off together in a sports car. Porsche, it was."

Larry French was still one step ahead of me, and not covering his tracks too well. I drained my beer and gave the bartender my card. "Would you ask him to call me anyway?"

"Sure. If he gets two jobs, he might pay his tab."

I went out onto the sidewalk and paused to button my coat. The rain had stopped, and there were faint blue patches overhead. So French and I had covered the same ground in an investigative conga line. What would he do next?

And, while I was on the subject, what *about* French? I hurried to my car and headed back to the Western Addition.

No one was at the front desk or in the parlor at Wintringham's. As I stood indecisively, I heard angry voices in the kitchen.

Arguments overheard on the sly can be very revealing. In

my occupation, I had long ago conquered my scruples against eavesdropping, as I had many other principles. I didn't rationalize; it was merely one of the things I had to do.

Now I crept down the hall toward a door which, I knew from my house tour, would lead to the breakfast room adjoining the kitchen. I pressed my ear against the door. Paul Collins' voice came through loud and clear.

". . . don't care if the project's in trouble! My inheritance was to be used for us, personally, not for business ventures!" His tone was high pitched.

"It's only a loan." Wintringham spoke soothingly. "If the project goes down the drain, so do we."

"I don't care! If you think I'm going to have my money used to benefit Larry French, you're mad!"

"It's not only for Larry's benefit, Paul. I know he's a sleazy character, but he's invested a lot in us. I can't kick him out to please you."

"Oh, that's right! You can't please me, but you want my money." There was the sound of a fist hitting wood. "You're not going to get it, David. The money is for us, not the business."

"Christ!" Wintringham's voice hardened. "Take a Valium before you fly off the handle, will you?"

"That's not funny, David. You know I'm nervous. First there's this killing. Now the business is about to fail." Collins began to whine. "You shouldn't make fun of me."

"I'm sorry. I shouldn't have. But Paul, don't you see, we've got to pull out of this somehow."

"Not with my money."

Wintringham sighed. "Think about it."

"My mind's made up."

"Think anyway." Footsteps went toward the dining room.

I rushed back down the hall and stood by the desk, trying to look as if I'd just come in. A moment later, Wintringham came out of the parlor, his bony shoulders drooping dispiritedly. The project must be in a great deal more trouble than he'd led me to believe.

He started when he saw me. "Sharon." He shook his head as if to clear it.

"Do you have time for a couple of questions?"

"Sure."

"Larry French—how long has he been your partner?"

"Around a year."

"And how much would you say he knows about construction work?"

Wintringham smiled faintly. "Very little. His contribution consists of running around and bullying the workers so they quit."

I nodded. It was beginning to fit. "Another thing. Do you have any lamps similar to the Cheshire Cat's Eye around? I mean, kerosene lamps?"

"There's one in the second parlor." He frowned. "But why?"

"It's occurred to me that I don't really know what a kerosene lamp looks like or how it works. In case I run across the Cheshire Cat's Eye, I'd like to know."

"Sure." He led me to the middle room, indicating a lamp with an etched-glass shade on top of an upright piano.

I examined it. "How does the kerosene go in?"

"You pour it here." He indicated an aperture. "And then you light it like so."

I watched, then mimicked the procedure.

"Does this mean you're likely to come across the lamp?" Wintringham asked.

"You never know."

"But it's so distinctive you wouldn't need to know what a kerosene lamp looked like to recognize it."

"You're probably right. I'm curious, that's all." I didn't want to tell him about the three electrified replicas, not yet. "One more request. May I use your phone?"

"Be my guest." He led me back to the hall and pointed out the instrument before he went upstairs.

I waited until he'd disappeared around the landing before

I dialed Ed's Place, the bar where Bob Keefer hung out. No, the barkeep told me, Bob hadn't come in. I called his aunt's house, but she said the same. Next I checked with my answering service. Johnny Hart had left a message. I dialed the number and got the restaurant owner.

"What's up?" I asked.

"Plenty. Raymond-the-Hit-Man's being held by the cops."

"What for?"

"Questioning on an assault. I got the word a couple of hours ago, so there's still time if you hurry."

"Time for what?"

Hart sighed. "Girl, you make some private eye. Now's your chance to go up against Nick Dettman. With Raymond on the loose, Dettman's dangerous, but alone he'll cave in like the chocolate-covered marshmallow he is."

I smiled at the metaphor. "What if he's not alone?"

"He's alone. I checked it out. He's at his office, and everybody else is gone for the day."

"Good work!"

"So get over there. But, girl, you be careful. Raymond's got a good lawyer; he's likely to be sprung any time now. And Dettman ain't exactly right in the head. You can't tell what he'll do. You take that gun, you hear?"

"I hear. And, Johnny—thanks."

"Don't mention it. I hate scum that push women around."

I hung up and paused, wondering why Hart was being so helpful. It could be a setup. Then I shrugged and headed for my car, patting the .38 in my bag.

19

This time I parked directly in front of Dettman's law office. Hefting my shoulder bag, where my gun rested within easy reach, I got out and approached the orange door.

Dettman sat slumped at his desk, thumbing through what

looked like a government pamphlet. He closed it, tossed it aside, and picked up another. I stepped inside, shutting the door behind me.

Dettman looked up. He blinked and straightened in his chair.

"Good afternoon, Mr. Dettman."

He wet his lips. "Where you get off coming here?"

"I wanted to ease your mind about my health. Since I haven't been around all day, you must have worried that Raymond overdid it. I know you'd never intentionally hurt anyone."

He swept the pamphlets aside. "Lady, I don't know what you're talking about."

"Then I'll explain." I sat down on the corner of his desk and took out my gun.

Dettman stared at it, his mouth half opening.

"Don't panic," I said. "I would never intentionally hurt anyone either."

Blindly Dettman reached out and felt around on the desk. I found the box of Fig Newtons and shoved it toward him. "Have a cookie, Mr. Dettman. It'll make you feel better."

He looked from the box to me, his full lips trembling. Johnny Hart had been right: Dettman was caving in like a chocolate-covered marshmallow in the heat of a campfire. I regarded him silently. His eyes flicked to the gun and back to my face.

"I am willing," I said, "to forgive and forget certain things. Raymond scared me, but he didn't really hurt me. So I have a deal for you."

At the word "deal," Dettman's eyes flashed with hopeful interest.

"I will forget about Raymond in exchange for information," I went on. "You will provide that information and, when Raymond is released by the police, you will tell him to leave me alone."

"What information?" Dettman's voice was hoarse.

"Let's start with the Cheshire Cat's Eye."

"The what?"

"Don't play dumb, Mr. Dettman."

"I'm not. What's this about a cat?"

"Not a cat, a lamp. A Tiffany lamp with a leaded-glass shade. Autumn leaves. A grinning mouth. One big yellow-green eye. Remember it?"

Comprehension and fear flooded his features. "That thing!"

"Yes. I presume Raymond delivered it to you?"

Dettman glanced at a large steel cabinet.

"Ah, you have it here."

He was silent.

"Go over there and get it." I motioned with my gun.

He sat still, his hand creeping toward the cookie box.

"Get it!"

Reluctantly, he went. The cardboard carton sat on the floor of the cabinet. Dettman placed it on the desk.

"Open it," I ordered.

With unsteady hands, he removed the lamp from its wrappings. I sucked in my breath. This was indeed the original. The autumnal colors glowed so richly that I didn't need the absence of a cord to tell the difference from Prince Albert's replicas.

"Quite a find, Mr. Dettman," I said. "Sit down and tell me why you went to such lengths to get it."

He eased his paunchy body into the chair. "No way, lady. I never heard of that thing until that slack-assed Raymond dragged it into my place last night. If that's what you're after, you go on and take it. It don't matter to me." In his agitation, his polished tones fell away and were replaced by the language of the ghetto.

"Oh, come on," I said, "don't give me that. Everybody I run into lately is after that lamp in one way or another. You're no exception."

He gestured helplessly. "I tell you, I don't want the damned thing. You take it."

"If that's true, then why did Raymond bring it to you?"

"You were ass up in the debris box after it. Raymond sees that, so he figures it's important, maybe it's got to do with Jake Kaufmann. So he figures I should have it."

"Why?"

"Why? That's the way Raymond operates. Ask him why."

"Okay," I said, taking another tack, "why did you send Raymond after me in the first place?"

Dettman groaned and buried his face in his hands.

"Why?"

"All right." He looked up, resigned. "I'll tell you the whole thing. But we got a deal, right? I tell you, you forget about Raymond?"

"Okay, a deal. Start at the beginning."

"The gun—you gonna put that down?"

"No, I'm not. The beginning, Mr. Dettman."

He sighed and leaned back, clasping his hands over his paunch. "Okay. It was Saturday. Saturday morning. I was here going over some papers. Larry French, Wintringham's partner, he came in."

"French? What did he want?"

"Their restoration project." Dettman smiled unpleasantly. "I could of told him. You don't move in on the people's territory, you don't expect to make over those buildings to force the black man out. But French, he's not so smart. Now their fancy restoration project's going down the tubes and French, he's scared this murder will put it under."

"So why did he discuss this with you, of all people? He's not stupid enough to think you'd help them."

"There's help and there's help." Dettman reached for a cookie and popped it into his mouth.

"Go on."

Around a mouthful of crumbs, he said, "French heard I knew someone who could fix things."

"Raymond."

"Right. He wanted me to get up something with Raymond for him."

"What?"

"He had in mind Raymond torching the restoration project."

I stared.

"They carry heavy fire insurance over there," Dettman added.

"Arson."

"Right."

"Good lord." French seemed more the villain of the piece every minute. If he collected on the fire insurance, he'd at least recoup his initial investment. But what of Wintringham? Was he in on the sabotage scheme? I thought of the argument I'd overheard between him and Collins, about Collins investing his inheritance in the business. No, I decided, French had acted on his own.

Dettman popped another cookie.

"So you contacted Raymond," I said.

"Yeah. He came over Saturday night, right after you left. He thought he could handle it."

"And, on top of that, you told him to handle me."

Dettman was silent.

"Let me ask you this: Did you send him after me on impulse, because you were angry when I left here that night?"

"Yeah." Dettman stared resolutely at the desk.

"Not very smart, for a man in your position. What happened next?"

"It was Sunday afternoon before I talked to French again. He hunted me up at my place."

"What did he want?"

"To call off the sabotage."

"Why?"

Dettman shrugged. "He said he'd found a better way to cut his losses."

A better way to cut his losses. That meant he'd either found a way to save the project or an alternate source of cash. Which?

"So you called Raymond off?"

"Not exactly. I left word in the usual places, but he didn't turn up until . . ."

"Until after he'd pushed me around."

Dettman stuffed another cookie into his mouth. "Right," he mumbled, spraying crumbs.

"Will Raymond follow your orders and forget about French's plan?"

Dettman looked surprised. "Sure. Why would he bother? Raymond works for money, not for kicks."

I didn't know whether I should be glad of that or not.

I stood up. "Put the lamp back in the carton, please."

He complied.

"Now carry it to the door."

He did, walking inches in front of the muzzle of my gun. I unlocked the car door. "Now set it down inside."

As he set it down, I stepped around him, pocketing the gun so no one on the street could see it. "Don't forget the second condition of our deal, Dettman. Tell Raymond to leave me alone."

The former city supervisor looked beaten and broken. "I said I would, didn't I? Just get yourself and that goddamn lamp out of my sight."

I was only too glad to do so.

20

As I drove away, my accelerator foot began to tremble and I had to pull back to the curb. I leaned on the steering wheel, my head on my arms, trying to control the attack of nerves.

The confrontation with Dettman had been a risk—a bigger risk than I'd wanted to admit when I went in there. And, although again I hadn't acknowledged it to myself at the time, during our entire conversation I'd been straining to hear Raymond's returning footsteps, steeling to defend myself against the two men.

Well, I thought, raising my head and smiling faintly, I pulled it off. Sharon McCone, ex-cheerleader and homecoming princess, can get tough when she wants to.

Secretly I wondered if I would have come on so strong had Dettman not been such a pushover.

My tremors conquered, I set off out Mission Street to look again for Bob Keefer. He could provide a vital link in the chain.

The pickup still stood in the driveway, tennis shoes with rips in the toes protruding from under it. I stopped alongside and called out the carpenter's name. A muffled voice greeted me.

I explained who I was. A more prolonged mumble answered, and then blue-jeaned legs emerged, followed by a torso and a head. Keefer had curly black hair, a stubbled chin, and vague eyes. Drugs, I decided. Downers, or maybe grass.

"My aunt gave me your card," Keefer said, raking his fingers through his unruly curls. "You got a job for me?"

"No." I took out the photostat of my private investigator's license and flashed it at him. It wasn't a police badge, but it was damned official looking, and I didn't think Keefer would question it.

He stared, swallowed, and glanced around furtively.

"Where can we talk?" I asked.

Keefer was silent. I followed his gaze to the window of his aunt's house, where a curtain moved slightly.

"You want to go to Ed's Place?" I suggested.

"Shit, no!" he exclaimed. "I got friends there. You think I want them to know about this?"

Clearly, he had something on his conscience. "Where, then?"

He motioned at the pickup. "In there. It don't run, but it's private."

I climbed into the passenger seat, and Keefer got behind the wheel. The upholstery was ripped, and beer cans littered the floor.

Keefer lit a cigarette. "So what's the beef?"

"It begins with a Tiffany lamp and a gentleman named Larry French."

He drew on the cigarette with elaborate nonchalance. "I never heard of them."

I leaned toward him. "Item number one: You sold the lamp

to a Salem Street junk dealer in October. There's a receipt to prove it. Item number two: French came to see you today and took you for a spin in his Porsche."

"You're nuts, lady."

"There are witnesses. Did French bother to tell you item number three?"

"What's that?"

"The lamp is a key piece of evidence in a murder case."

His lips twitched and he gripped the steering wheel. "Murder?"

"Yes. Now talk!" McCone gets tough again.

"I . . . Oh, Jesus! What murder? What're you talking about?"

"Three years ago, a man named Richard Wintringham was killed during a burglary. The lamp was one of the things taken. Let's hear where you got it, as well as the other stuff."

"Wintringham?" His jaw went slack. "I worked for a David Wintringham, but I never heard of this Richard guy."

"He was David's father."

"Oh, Jesus." He was silent for a moment. "The way it was, I was working on this job, tearing out a lot of shit in an old house that had been converted to apartments."

"Where?"

"On Steiner Street. Wintringham and Associates was the general on the job."

"And?"

"And I'm ripping out the sheetrock from around an old fireplace that was walled up, and I look in there, and there's all this stuff. A lamp, a clock, bottles, a lot of shit that looked like it might be worth something."

"So you took it."

"No way!" He drew himself up indignantly. "I don't take chances like that. I got a reputation to protect in the trade. Nope, what I did was box it up and drag it over to one of the partners, Larry French. He wasn't interested in it, told me I could have it if I wanted. So I threw it in the truck and about a month later,

I was short on cash on account of Wintringham running out of money and laying me off. So I sold it to a couple of places on Salem Street. And that's that.''

I thought of the fireplace in the Stick-style house on Steiner. ''Which house was this in?''

''Beige stucco one, two doors down from Wintringham's. Fireplace is in the front room.''

''You seem pretty definite about that.''

''I should be. Today . . .'' He stopped.

''Today what?''

''Nothing.'' He crushed out his cigarette and reached for another. ''That's the story.''

''Not quite. What did French want today?''

''French? I haven't seen him in months.''

''Shall I get your aunt out here to verify that you went off with him? Or the bartender at Ed's?''

''Jesus!'' He glanced at the window of the house. The curtain was still pulled out of place. ''Lady, I can't tell you.''

''Why not?''

''French, he paid me.'' A crafty glint came into his vague eyes. ''I got to make repairs on the truck, you see, and after that there's the rent. I'm behind. Now, if you would help me out on the rent . . .''

I sighed. ''How much do you owe?''

''Three months. That's only a hundred and fifty altogether. It's a cheap room.''

''I'll give you one month's worth now. If the information leads to Wintringham's killer, you'll get the rest.'' Thank God I had cashed a check recently.

''I don't know.'' Keefer frowned. ''How do I know I can trust you?''

''You don't. But it's either trust me or talk to Homicide. They'll hold you until you talk for free.''

''Bitch!''

''Name-calling won't get you the fifty dollars. Talking will.''

''You promise the rest later?''

''If your information helps me.''

"Okay. French gave me five hundred, but every little bit helps." He sighed with great resignation. "Okay. He came here this morning and asked about the lamp. I told him what I did with it. Then he said he was just checking, to see how truthful I was. He already knew what happened to the stuff, and he showed me one of the bottles to prove it. He wanted to know exactly where and how I'd found the stuff—he didn't ask for the details before, thought it was in a corner of the basement or maybe the attic of that house."

"So you told him about the fireplace."

"Yeah."

"Then what?"

"He took me over there in his Porsche—man, that's one tasty car—and had me show him the fireplace and how the stuff was setting inside."

"And?"

"And he gave me the five hundred bucks to forget I'd ever heard of it. He said he might have a job for me when something came up." Keefer's mouth drooped. "I don't suppose he will, if you nail him for murder, huh?"

"Probably not." But I doubted French was a murderer. Something close, but not a killer.

"Shit!" Keefer struck the steering wheel with his open palm. "Nothing ever goes right for me."

"You got French's five hundred. And your rent will be taken care of."

"Yeah, but I still won't have a job. And I'll probably end up in court putting the finger on French. Shit! I got no luck."

I wasn't about to debate the point. "How *was* the stuff arranged in the fireplace, Bob?"

"Careful, like it was a little room in a dollhouse. The lamp was in the middle, with the clock on one side and a silver thing on the other. And the bottles were lined up in front. I remember thinking at the time that somebody had been real gentle with them, like maybe they wanted to keep them safe."

I frowned. French? That definitely ruled him out. He wouldn't care. He'd been willing to give them away to a workman. And Charmaine had said he'd had no conception of the Cheshire Cat's Eye's worth.

"Yeah," Keefer mused, "I remember thinking it was strange, why anybody would take so much trouble."

21

Why, indeed?

I turned the question over in my mind as I wrestled with the front-door lock of my apartment building, lugging the Cheshire Cat's Eye under my arm.

Why secrete objects away so carefully, rather than destroy or dispose of them?

I entered the apartment building. The lobby was pitch black. As the door shut behind me, a burly figure loomed out from under the stairs.

I flattened against the wall and reached for my gun.

The figure kept coming. I clicked off the safety.

A flashlight came on. The figure advanced on me, carrying a package of light bulbs.

I laughed weakly in relief.

Tim O'Riley, my kindly, beer-guzzling building manager, looked quizzically at me. "Oh, it's you. What the hell's so funny?"

I slipped the gun back in my bag. "Nothing. You startled me, that's all. I thought you were a mugger."

"Gee, thanks. Hold this, will you?" He extended the flashlight.

I trained it on the wall sconce as Tim screwed in the bulb. The light came on, illuminating the faded turquoise carpet and the little bed of plastic geraniums the owner had planted to beautify the otherwise undistinguished lobby.

"One of the tenants has been stealing the bulbs." Tim took the flashlight from me and went over to another empty sconce.

"It doesn't surprise me."

"Between that and your cat using those fake flowers for a litter box, I've got my work cut out for me. Of course," he added, "the cat shows good sense. What kind of a person would put in a thing like that anyway?"

"The same kind who would spray the ceilings with that sparkly paint."

"Yeah. Say, your phone's been ringing off the hook for the last half hour. Guess you haven't trained the cat to answer."

"Damn! The answering service is supposed to pick it up. Well, I'm here now." I unlocked my door, mulling over the vagaries of my service. My friend Claudia owned it and gave me a break on the twenty-four-hour rate, which I very much appreciated. I did not, however, appreciate her succession of inept daytime and early-evening operators. The efficient Claudia preferred to take the late-night shift, when she could engage in protracted philosophical conversations with clients who could not sleep.

I went down the long inner hall to the main room of my studio apartment. The building was nineteen-twenties vintage and shared some characteristics with Victorians: high-coved ceilings, nice hardwood floors, and softly angled bay windows which, unfortunately in this case, overlooked an alley.

There, any resemblance between my apartment and Wintringham's dream houses stopped. My furniture had clean, modern lines and well-grained light wood. The rugs were in earth tones and clear and bright accenting colors. The white walls were covered with my amateur efforts at photography in plain Plexiglas frames. My only concession to the past, in fact, was the quilts on the bed, which my grandmother had made.

It was home, my refuge from the often-rough world I operated in, and I loved it.

Now I removed the Cheshire Cat's Eye from its box and set it on the bureau. Strangely, it did not look out of place among the modern objects. Maybe I should pick up a few good old pieces.

I went to the kitchen and got a glass of wine from my other antique, the electrified icebox that was built into the wall. It was one of the less convenient features of the apartment, because it operated off a compressor in the basement. Tim was supposed to notify all the tenants on the day when he turned off the compressor so the iceboxes could defrost, but invariably I wasn't home at the time. Over the years, I had gotten used to returning to have all my groceries wash out the icebox door at me.

Returning to the main room, I sat cross-legged on the bed, staring at the Tiffany lamp. The eye held a mocking light. The teeth smirked at me.

"Don't look so smart," I told it. "I'll solve this one yet."

French. Larry French. He had once killed a man with his bare hands. He had had the Cheshire Cat's Eye in his possession, according to Charmaine. He didn't know enough about construction to fake an accident properly.

French had wanted to sabotage Wintringham's restoration project, ostensibly to recoup his initial investment in what he saw as a sure disaster. What other reason could he have for ordering the arson? To cover up something? Destroy evidence? Evidence of what?

And why had French paid Bob Keefer to keep silent about the objects in the fireplace if he hadn't put them there? But if he had, why ask Keefer to show him how they were arranged? And would French have arranged them so carefully anyway? No. Who, then?

David Wintringham would have. But would he have killed his own father? Hard to believe; the affection there seemed to have been genuine, if ambivalent.

Paul Collins, then. But Wintringham had alibied him for the night of both murders. Would Wintringham do that for him, if his lover had killed his father? Doubtful. Besides, Collins didn't care about Victorian antiques. Look at his kitchen. And what had he said to me? That in Dayton they had nice old houses, but they didn't make such a fuss over them.

Who *would* care about the objects? Charmaine.

But what motive would she have for doing in old man Wintringham? Jake's killing was clearly a coverup, but why Wintringham? There was no apparent reason, and certainly none to link Charmaine with it. And wouldn't it take more strength than the tiny decorator possessed?

Eleanor van Dyne. She was certainly strong enough, but ditto the lack of motive. But hadn't Prince Albert said she had her reasons for keeping out of the controversy that swirled around the Cheshire Cat's Eye? What were they? I'd have to find out.

Prince Albert. After verifying his story about buying the lamp from Charlie Cornish, I was inclined to discount him. Unless there was something I didn't know.

Nick Dettman. The same.

Johnny Hart. I didn't want to believe ill of the restaurant proprietor. And that was dangerous.

Raymond-the-Hit-Man. Merely a neighborhood thug.

My big black-and-white cat, Watney, entered by the fire-escape window. He came up to have his ears scratched, then trotted off toward the kitchen and—what else—food.

So back to French. Maybe he was the killer. He drank a good bit, which none of my other suspects seemed to do. While I had discounted him because of his capacity, it all depended on your definition of drunkenness. Jake's may have been broader than mine.

I didn't like French for the killer, though. I could see him as a blackmailer. All his movements lately pointed that way. After all, he'd found a "better way to cut his losses." To me, that suggested he knew who the murderer was and hoped to cash in on it.

Yes, if I could get French to reveal that knowledge, the case would be solved. But I didn't believe in making a grandstand play at the risk of blowing everything. It would be better to let the police handle him. It was time to take the facts to Greg.

I sipped wine and smiled smugly, picturing the lieutenant's surprise. While his men had gone snooping in culverts and trash-cans for a bloody hammer, I'd uncovered details leading straight to the killer. While they'd tediously interviewed every neighborhood resident, I'd cut to the heart of the matter . . .

The phone rang. I snatched it up.

"Sharon?" Wintringham's voice trembled on the edge of hysteria. "Where have you been?"

"What's wrong?"

"Can you come over here right away? There's more trouble and I've got no one—"

"What's happened?"

"It's simply terrible!"

"What! What is?"

"It's Larry French. He's been murdered in one of our houses!"

22

When I arrived at Steiner Street, the red and blue lights of the patrol cars pulsed, bouncing off the high retaining wall and throwing the tangled vegetation into eerie relief against the facades of the Victorians. The excitement centered on the Stick-style house where I'd first met Wintringham and Charmaine on Saturday. Strange: I'd automatically assumed the big Queen Anne would again be the death house.

I glanced up the street and noted Greg's BMW, double-parked by a patrol car. His position in the department was that of administrator, working the day shift, pulling all the elements of investigations together, but it was not in his character to confine himself to a desk job. He personally visited as many of the crime scenes as possible, and was on call twenty-four hours a day.

A crowd of spectators, most of them black, milled about at the foot of the stairway in the wall. Wintringham was nowhere in sight. I pushed through the crowd toward the uniformed officer who guarded the steps. He wasn't likely to let me pass. I glanced around for a solution to the problem and spotted Inspector Gallagher.

Gallagher was an owlish young man whose frank admiration

on the few occasions we'd run across each other had made my day. I waved to him, and he came over.

"Hi," I said. "Is the lieutenant inside?"

"Yeah. They're about to bring the body out. You on the case?"

"Yes. Could you take me up there? I need to talk to him."

"Sure." Gallagher slipped a hand under my elbow and led me past the uniformed man. Branches and blackberry vines brushed against me as we approached the house.

Inside, the scene was reminiscent of Friday night, the front parlor garishly illuminated by portable floodlights. The body, however, was covered and strapped to a stretcher, and white-coated ambulance attendants stood by, awaiting the go-ahead. I breathed more easily; dead bodies held no attraction for me.

Glancing around the room, I spotted Greg talking with one of his inspectors. His tall, confident presence, coupled with the memory of the last time I'd seen him, gave me a rush of pleasure. I sucked my breath in, reminding myself of where I was and why I was here.

Apparently *my* presence provoked no similar response in Greg. He saw me, and his dark eyebrows came together in a scowl. Turning abruptly from the inspector, he strode across the room and grabbed my arm.

"What the hell are you doing here?" he growled.

I tried to peel his fingers off my arm, but it didn't work. "I'm on the case."

"The hell you are! I can't stop you from snooping around for Wintringham, but I'll be damned if I'm admitting you to a crime scene. How'd you get in, anyway?"

I glanced at Gallagher. He looked confused and apprehensive. Not wanting to get him in trouble, I merely said, "Subterfuge."

"You've read too goddamned many of those detective novels." Greg looked at Gallagher too, but his expression, rather than one of anger, was of sympathy.

I wrenched free of Greg and surveyed the room. Charmaine's paint and wallpaper samples lay on the floor where she had left them on Saturday, but now they were splattered with blood and some other material—brain tissue?—that I wasn't sure I cared to identify. "The same MO, huh?" I said. "Did you find the weapon this time?"

Greg merely glared at me.

My eyes rested on the fireplace. The sheetrock had been pulled completely off, exposing its cracked tiles, dirty cement hearth, and a single pressed-glass bottle. I started, and took a step forward.

Greg didn't notice my surprise, but he did notice the motion. He clapped his hand firmly on my shoulder and spun me around.

"Thank you for coming," he said in a tone of exaggerated politeness. "Gallagher, will you please show Ms. McCone to her car? She needs to go home and get her beauty rest." He shoved me toward the inspector and turned on his heel.

"Sorry," I muttered to Gallagher.

He shrugged and led me outside. "I didn't realize he'd react like that."

"Neither did I. Live and learn." My feelings were hurt, but not very much. It had been worth the rebuff to see that bottle in the fireplace. I ran down the stairway in the retaining wall, leaving Gallagher to contemplate his boss's complexities.

I sped down the sidewalk to Wintringham's house. A police guard took my name in, then admitted me. I went into the parlor.

The tableau there warred with the prim loveliness of the room: Paul Collins in bathrobe and slippers, looking pasty and sick; Wintringham in workshirt and ripped jeans, his paint-splattered boots propped on the fragile coffee table; Charmaine, her suede jumpsuit smeared with blood, her eyes puffy, hair tangled.

She looked up and made a sound that was close to a whimper.

Paul's lips trembled, but he said nothing.

Wintringham glanced at me indifferently. His eyes had the glaze that comes from shock. "Oh, there you are," he said flatly. "It took you long enough."

I sat on the couch. "What happened?"

"That should be obvious. Someone murdered Larry."

"Who found him?"

Charmaine cleared her throat and ran her hands over her bloodstained thighs.

"Charmaine did," Wintringham said. "She came over tonight to pick up her samples. He was . . ."

"He was lying there. The blood. All around him. On my samples." Her words were sing-song and shrill. "I tried to wake him. I held his head. His ugly head." She buried her face in her hands.

Surprisingly, Collins was the one who moved. He knelt beside her, putting his arm around her shoulders. "Don't think about it now. You'll feel better if you don't think."

Charmaine sobbed.

Wintringham stood and motioned me into the hall.

"When did she find him?" I asked in a low voice.

"About two hours ago. She came running in here, screaming. I went down there. It was like she said. Larry was lying there, with blood all over the place. His head was caved in."

"And you called the police?"

"Yes. And tried to call you." The words were accusing. Wintringham leaned against the newel post, his arms folded across his bony chest. "Sharon, I'm afraid for Charmaine."

"You ought to get a doctor over here. A sedative would help."

"That's not it." He shook his head. "I'm afraid the police think she killed Larry."

"What?"

"One of the inspectors questioned us. He acted like he didn't believe Charmaine's story. And then Paul inadvertently let it slip that she and Larry had quarreled on Saturday."

"Oh, terrific!"

"He didn't mean to incriminate her. And, besides, they would have found out anyway; there was quite a blowup when he took off from the trade show with that blonde. Everyone there heard it."

"Tell me, David," I said, "do *you* believe her?"

He hesitated. "I don't know. She came in here with blood all over her. And there was no reason she had to pick up those samples tonight. And they did quarrel. Charmaine has a bad temper . . ." His voice trailed off disspiritedly.

I considered the little decorator. How far would French have had to push her before that temper snapped? But, if my gut-level feeling was correct, this murder and Jake Kaufmann's *and* Richard Wintringham's had all been committed by the same person. Wintringham's death, for whatever reason, had been the start of it all, and the Cheshire Cat's Eye was the key. That, and the pressed-glass bottle in the fireplace.

"How well did Charmaine know your father?" I asked.

Wintringham's dull eyes flickered. "Quite well. She was one of his protégés."

"How so?"

"My father, in spite of his limitations as an architect, admired excellence. Charmaine was the daughter of one of his draftsmen, and she'd shown a talent for design. My father sent her to school and then got her a job with a good firm here. When I went into business, she quit and came to work for me."

"How would you describe her relations with your father? Were they affectionate? Cordial? Or . . . ?"

He drew himself up. "What are you trying. . . . Come on, Sharon!"

"It's better we talk about it now, before the police start asking."

Wintringham glanced at his watch. "We don't have much time, either. That inspector said his lieutenant would be here as soon as they finish at the crime scene."

His lieutenant. Greg was taking a very personal interest in this case. Judging from his earlier reception of me, I'd better not be here when he arrived. "Okay. What kind of terms was Charmaine on with your father?"

"As good as could be expected."

"Which means what?"

"My father was a very domineering man. If he paid for a

person's education, he expected to have a hand in guiding her career."

"He tried to tell Charmaine what to do?"

"He told her where to work. She hated the firm, but she worked there. He told her where to live, and she obeyed him. He even told her who to see socially. When I came back from New York, he tried to match us up. I'm afraid I was quite a disappointment to him." He smiled wryly.

"So he really attempted to control her entire life."

"And he succeeded."

"To some extent."

Wintringham shifted uneasily against the newel post. "Totally."

"No." I shook my head. "Not totally. His death set her free."

23

Eleanor van Dyne's house sat deep in Pacific Heights, on the edge of the Presidio. Surprisingly, it was not a Victorian, but a two-story ell-shaped block that must have been daringly modern thirty years ago. I stood on the sidewalk, unable to reconcile it with its owner's zeal for the city's dowager ladies, as I'd come to think of the Victorians. Behind it, a fine mist blew in from the Golden Gate, curling through the eucalyptus and Monterey pine of the army base. It was the kind of mist that would burn off quickly with the June morning, leaving the city clean and shining. Nevertheless, I shivered as I walked toward the lights of van Dyne's house.

A maid in a black uniform and white apron answered my ring and informed me that the van Dynes were giving a dinner party. Her expression indicated I would not be welcome in that company.

"I think she'll see me." I fished out one of my cards and wrote Richard Wintringham's name on it. A ghost from the past seemed an unsuitable way to gain entry to such a house, but I was certain it would work. In minutes, footsteps sounded on the slate floor of the foyer, and van Dyne appeared, attired in a simple black cocktail dress and pearls, looking surprisingly like the maid, minus the apron. Her face was a smooth mask, but the hand in which she held my card trembled.

"What do you mean, coming here at this hour?" she demanded. "Don't you know to make an appointment?"

I knew all about appointments and avoided them whenever possible. If you called ahead, it gave people a chance to think up a story.

"Larry French was murdered in the stuccoed-over Stick in the Steiner Street block tonight."

Van Dyne caught her lower lip between her teeth.

"I thought you should know."

"Which house, did you say?"

"The beige stucco Stick. The one where you talked with David and Charmaine on Saturday morning."

She nodded.

"The police will probably arrest Charmaine for it."

"Charmaine?" She frowned. "Did she kill him?"

"I don't know. That's why I'm here; you can help me."

"You want me to implicate Charmaine?"

"I want you to help me uncover the truth."

She laughed harshly. "Is that all you're interested in, the truth?"

"At the moment, yes."

"And why do you think I can help?"

"Prince Albert came to you about the Cheshire Cat's Eye. He said you, of all people, could identify it. He also said you had your reasons for staying out of the investigation of Richard Wintringham's death."

Van Dyne glanced down at the card in her hand, then over her shoulder, toward the sound of convivial voices. "I see. All right, come with me."

She led me to a deeply carpeted stairway and up, to a wide

hall. The walls were decorated with modern paintings, and occasional sidetables held pieces of sculpture that looked like originals. Again, I wondered about van Dyne and this house. Had the financier husband chosen and decorated it?

The question was answered in the affirmative by the sitting room to which she took me. Its soft light came from wall sconces that once might have been fitted for gas. Its furniture was ornate, its wallpaper embossed in rich red. In a corner, on a table, stood a Victorian dollhouse.

I moved closer to it. The tower and gables were strikingly familiar. "It's—"

"Yes, it's a replica of Richard's house." She stood looking at it, her hands calmly folded in front of her. Upon entering this room, which obviously was her private domain, her agitation had vanished. "He had it made for me, long ago."

"Then you were . . ."

"We were lovers, for over twenty years. Please, sit down."

I took a chair from which I could see both her and the dollhouse. "Is this common knowledge?"

She smiled gently. In the soft light of the sconces, she seemed young and serene. "In preservationist circles, yes. You can't be together that long without the fact becoming known."

"But what about . . . ?" I gestured downward at the first floor.

"Well, yes." She sighed. "Some of my husband's and my friends know. As I said, it's difficult to keep a secret for twenty years. But William? No. He is well protected by a tacit conspiracy of silence. *Most* people honor that." Her mouth twitched at the stressed word.

"Is that why you dropped your lawsuit against Jake Kaufmann? Because he blackmailed you by threatening to tell your husband?"

Van Dyne looked genuinely shocked. She patted her gray-blond coif. "Oh, no, dear. I wouldn't call it blackmail. Jake and I merely talked over the unfairness of my suit, and the unfairness to William, should he find out about my liaison."

Jake stoop to blackmail? At first it shocked me. But then, if I considered how much he prized his work, maybe it was more believable. After all, van Dyne's suit had threatened his professional reputation, his livelihood. And in her genteel world, one wouldn't call what Jake had threatened blackmail. Clever of him to realize that. "I guess it would have hurt your husband very much had he found out."

Again, she looked surprised. "Hurt? I doubt it. He would have been humiliated, though. William is a man of taste, as you can tell from this house. He would be horrified to know that his wife had carried on an affair with the Wintringham row houses."

"Good lord." I had a great deal to learn about the upper levels of society.

"I'm sorry?"

"Never mind. What kind of a man was Richard Wintringham?"

Her face softened. "A good man. Like William, a man of taste, in spite of the row houses. He built them for the present, but he lived in a more gracious past."

"I've heard that he could be ruthless and domineering."

"That too." Apparently she saw no dichotomy there.

"Did you know David well?"

"Not really. David's mother died when the boy was ten. His father didn't know what to do with him, so he sent him East to prep school and then college. We were very discreet when he was home on vacations; it wouldn't have done for a young boy to know about us."

"But he must have realized later."

"Yes, but it was after the fact. Richard and I were seeing less of one another. He was growing old, and our relationship became platonic. After college, David remained in the East, in New York, for a number of years. By the time he returned here to live, we'd broken . . ." She stopped, listening to her words.

"You'd broken off? Quarreled?"

She picked at an imaginary piece of lint on her black dress. "Not a quarrel. We had differences."

"About?"

"When a man grows old, often he becomes foolish."

"And how did Richard Wintringham express this foolishness?"

She looked solemnly at me for a long moment. "Charmaine."

"Was he in love with her?"

"Oh, I wouldn't say love." She gestured helplessly. "It was more of an infatuation. He knew he couldn't have her, so instead he tried to run her life. He made the poor girl miserable. He got her a job at the firm he deemed suitable and was always calling her employer to check on her progress. He insisted she take the apartment he found for her. He tried to rule her romantic life. It was a great price to pay for an education."

"And you fought with him over it?"

"Not fought. I advised. He listened and did what he wanted anyway." Van Dyne's eyes were far away, on the model of Richard Wintringham's mansion. "He was a fool, and a hard man to get along with. But he was also a good man. He'd merely come to live more and more in the past, when men could rule all they touched."

"So you broke with him over Charmaine?"

"I saw less of him, for a while. But then he had a heart attack and needed someone to look after him. I was in and out of there that whole spring, supervising his servants, seeing that he had the little things he needed."

"Which spring was that?"

Van Dyne directed her oddly innocent eyes at me. "Why, the spring he died. It was a lovely spring; we'd never seen better. The days were warm and clear; the whole city was sunshine and pastels. The lilacs bloomed in Richard's yard; their smell was everywhere. The loveliness was such a contrast to what was happening there on Steiner Street. It made everything seem all the more terrible."

"What things?"

"Richard was ill, of course. He looked gray and weak. I knew he hadn't much more time left. And David had returned from New York with Paul Collins and stashed him in that little

Stick where Larry French was killed tonight. Richard was desperately trying to match Charmaine up with David—I guess he had decided if he couldn't have her, his son should."

"Didn't he realize David was gay?"

"Not immediately. When he did, he was livid. I was afraid he would have another heart attack. Poor Richard." She shook her head. "Nothing was going his way. There he was, trying to arrange a marriage for his son, and all the time David was in love with another man and Charmaine was in love with Prince Albert."

"Prince Albert? There's nothing between them now, is there?"

"Oh, no, dear. That was over long ago. For their romance to have withstood the dominance of Richard Wintringham it would have taken more devotion than either of them felt."

I stared at van Dyne, then turned my gaze to the dollhouse. It seemed peopled with miniature figures: the old man in his tower study, trying to rule lives; van Dyne running in and out with little gifts for the invalid; David and Charmaine, meeting in the parlor and then going off, he to his lover down the street, and she to Prince Albert's Lighthouse.

The figures breathed, moved, and spoke within the confines of the dollhouse. And then they vanished one by one as the pieces of my case fell together.

24

The pieces were still falling into place as I drove home to my apartment on Guerrero Street. The trouble was, they weren't falling fast enough.

I sat down at my desk, ignoring Watney's pleas for food, tapping my fingers on the base of the phone and staring at the Cheshire Cat's Eye.

Three murders. The initial one, three years ago. What motive? I'd have to find the killer and ask him.

A second murder, last Friday night. Jake Kaufmann had gotten too close to the truth. He'd confronted the killer with the replica of the lamp. Fear of disclosure had caused Jake's death. Death by the hand of someone who was "usually tanked up."

Tanked up. But none of my suspects was a drunk. Tanked up . . .

Then the third murder, this evening. Larry French had seen a chance to profit from what he'd discovered over the last two days. The pressed-glass bottle in the fireplace, where it had originally been hidden, was a show-business-like pressure tactic. But it had backfired because French had underestimated his victim.

Why? Because the murderer was likely to be drunk?

The killings were getting closer together. Certainly now the killer could be pushed to a fourth murder—or to a confession. Didn't drunks tell the truth more often than not?

Tanked up. What if . . .

I sat up straighter, my fingers clutching the phone.

Of course. What if I'd misheard Jake? He was upset, not speaking clearly. Of course.

I snatched up the phone and tried to call Greg. The lieutenant was interrogating a suspect and could not take calls. I asked for Gallagher. The inspector had left. I hung up and glared across the room at the Tiffany lamp.

"We'll have to handle this alone, you and I," I told it. Glancing at my watch, I picked up the receiver again and called Charlie Cornish at his apartment over the new shop. He answered, sounding weary.

"Charlie," I said, "do you know where I can get some kerosene?"

"You do ask the damndest things. What do you want it for?"

"To fuel a lamp."

"Oh." There was a pause. "Some gas stations sell it, in fifty-gallon drums."

"Well, I certainly don't need that much!"

"You don't have to buy the whole drum, dummy. Still, I'd be hard pressed to tell you which station to try, and even if I could, they might not be open this late. Wait a second."

I heard the receiver clunk down and Charlie's footsteps shuffling away. It was several minutes before they returned.

"Just like I thought," he said. "Austin had some downstairs. He was testing out some old lamps he picked up at an auction. You're welcome to it."

"Great! I'll be right over."

I loaded the Cheshire Cat's Eye in my car, checked the gun in my purse, and headed for Valencia Street. Charlie met me on the sidewalk and handed the container of kerosene through the car window.

"You be careful with that stuff," he cautioned. "I don't want you burned."

"I'll take care. Thanks, Charlie."

"Yeah. Come back in one piece so you can fill me in on your shenanigans." As I drove off, I could see him in the rear-view mirror, still standing on the sidewalk, waving.

No police cars were in evidence at Steiner Street. When the San Francisco police finished with a crime scene, they finished fast. Still, I parked a block away and crept through the shadows, lugging the lamp and kerosene. The windows of the Victorians were dark. All the better for my purposes.

There was a police seal on the front door of the Queen Anne, and the lock looked sturdy. I set my burdens down and glanced around. Often old sash windows didn't work properly. I tested the one next to the porch and, sure enough, it wobbled up unevenly in its frame. Thrusting the lamp and kerosene in before me, I entered the front parlor. I closed the window and crouched below it, listening. There was no sound except for a car on the side street.

Pulling my flashlight from my purse, I made my way to the stairs and up to the tower room that had been Richard Wintringham's study, and his death place. Briefly, I shined the light around. The room was a rectangle, bowing out at the tower corner. The curved glass of its three windows was undraped. There were no furnishings, save for a few packing cases containing books. They would make an excellent table. I dragged them directly into the tower, then set the lamp on them and began to fill it, the way David Wintringham had shown me that afternoon.

Some of the kerosene spilled on my fingers, and the lamp filled slowly. I prayed I was doing it right. Finally I set the container down and extracted matches from my bag. The first three didn't work, but on the fourth it caught.

The lamp flared into brightness. I gasped at the rich reds and golds and greens. The cat's eye gleamed, and the teeth grinned conspiratorially at me. At last, they seemed to say, justice will be done.

Or would it? Would the killer see the light and come to investigate? How long would it take?

I crossed to the far side of the rectangle and crouched deep in the shadows, my back to the wall, my hand on my gun. It was cold in the tower. I had a knot in my stomach, and my limbs tingled with anticipation.

To calm myself, I began to sort through the facts.

An old man, who had tried to dominate everyone whose life had touched his, had died violently here. Why?

Because he'd tried to run one life too many.

Someone had tried to cover up the crime by faking a burglary, and had been successful for quite a while. Until what?

Until the stolen objects were discovered by a workman and sold to a junk shop. From which they were recovered. And reproduced.

Causing a second person to die.

And a third.

They had all died by the hand of the person who had so carefully placed those objects in the fireplace and walled it up again. Who?

A meticulous person, who liked order.

A person with money, susceptible to French's blackmail.

A person who, three years ago, had had access to that room with the fireplace . . .

Footsteps sounded below. I released the safety on my gun.

The steps came up the stairs, along the hall. They paused outside the door.

The killer stood in the shadows of the hallway, breathing hard.

I said, "Come all the way into the room, Paul."

25

Paul Collins stepped through the door. His moonlike face was white in the glow from the lamp. I remained in the shadows, by the high-manteled fireplace.

"Who's there?" He shielded his eyes from the glare and groped toward the lamp.

I didn't answer.

"Who's there?" Collins repeated. "I saw the light and came to investigate. Whose lamp is that?"

I moved between him and the door. "You can drop the act, Paul. You know whose it was."

He whirled around and peered into the gloom. "Sharon, is that you? What are you doing here?"

"Waiting for you to revisit the scene of your first crime."

"I don't understand." Pinpointing me by the sound of my voice, he took a step forward.

"Stay right there. I know you killed them, Paul."

"Killed who? Me, kill someone? Who?"

"Start with Richard Wintringham. He liked to dominate people. He all but wrecked Charmaine's life. He ruined Prince Albert's romance with her. I imagine he made David's life hell. For all her sentimentality, I'll bet he gave Eleanor van Dyne a lot of unhappiness too. I suspect even Jake Kaufmann suffered at his hands."

"Well, he wasn't the easiest person to get along with, but . . ."

"Yes, and all those people admit it. And they say that Richard Wintringham was furious when he found out about David and you. It made me wonder why you would say you liked him, that he was a nice man. I guess you figured it wouldn't do to bad-mouth your murder victim. It might have made someone suspicious."

Collins was silent.

"What did he say to you that night, Paul? Did he order you to stop seeing David?"

Again Collins took a step forward.

"Hold it," I cautioned.

"Oh, there you are." His eyes had adjusted to the dark. "Why don't we go back to the house and talk about this over a cup of tea?"

"No." I raised my gun higher.

Collins started. "Sharon, that isn't necessary!"

"What happened in this room that night, Paul?"

He licked his lips, eyes on the gun, and took several steps backward, into the tower.

I raised the gun still higher. "What happened, I asked."

Collins glanced around frantically.

"There's no way out, Paul."

His plump body sagged. He looked down at the floor and shuffled his feet. "You want to know what happened?" he asked brokenly. "He offered me money. *Money* to leave David alone. I told him I had my own money, that I couldn't be bought. He said he'd disinherit David. I knew how much these houses meant to David; even then he had plans to renovate the block."

"So you killed his father."

He retreated further into the tower. The glow of the Cheshire Cat's Eye touched his face. "First I tried to talk to him, to explain how I was good for David. He said . . . said no . . . faggot could possibly be good for his son." Collins closed his eyes. There were tears on his cheeks. "That's when I killed him. I've always had trouble with my temper; I take tranquilizers to control it. But that night, tranquilizers weren't enough."

Yes, tranquilizers. He got "tranqued up," like Jake had said. Not tanked, but tranqued. I felt a stab of pity for Collins but, like his tranquilizers that night, it wasn't enough. I said, "So you took the things in order to simulate a burglary and hid them in the fireplace at your apartment."

"Yes. It was easy; the sheetrock was already loose. If I had gotten rid of them, they might have been found, and then the police would have realized it wasn't a burglary. And I couldn't sell them; I might have been remembered and identified. As long as I lived in that apartment, they were safe. After I moved in with David, I was in terror that they'd be found and I kept meaning to go back for them, but . . ."

"When did you find out they were no longer in the fireplace?"

"Three or four months ago. I kept waiting for them to turn up, but they never did."

"Until Jake Kaufmann came to you with the replica of the Cheshire Cat's Eye he'd borrowed from Prince Albert. Did he try to blackmail you?"

Collins turned to look at the lamp. "Jake wouldn't have done that. He called for David and said he thought he knew who had the things that had been taken when Mr. Wintringham died. He said he needed to make sure, because it would implicate a good friend."

"Prince Albert. You took this call?"

Collins nodded, still staring at the lamp. "I told Jake that it would upset David too much to talk about it, but that I'd be willing to identify it. I suggested we meet here, in Mr. Wintringham's old house, because it might jog my memory."

"Surely your memory didn't need jogging."

Collins was silent.

"You planned to kill him, didn't you?"

"No!" He whirled to face me. "This was merely a place where David wasn't likely to come. That's all!"

Nice, how after three murders he could still delude himself. "Jake was convinced the lamp was a replica of the Cheshire Cat's Eye, wasn't he?"

"Yes. He'd only seen it once or twice, but when he brought the replica here, it jogged *his* memory. He insisted on taking it to the police. I couldn't risk that. We went downstairs, and I told him there was something I needed from the dining room. The hammer was on the mantel . . ."

"Why'd you fake the accident the way you did? I would think you'd know more about construction than that."

Collins hung his head. "I didn't. It was Larry. He admitted as much tonight. He saw me leave, although he didn't recognize me in the dark, and went in to see if everything was all right. When he found Jake, he panicked, thinking what a murder could do to the project. He faked the accident, not me."

And when that hadn't worked, he'd turned to Raymond-the-Hit-Man. "Larry also found the replica of the lamp, didn't he? It got broken in your struggle with Jake."

"Yes." Once again he looked over at the Cheshire Cat's Eye, as if mesmerized by its deep colors. "I should have taken it with me, but I just ran. Larry took it home and, when he heard you and David talking about it, he connected it with the stuff he'd given the workman and traced it. Then he fit everything together."

"And arranged to meet you in the fireplace room in order to blackmail you. The bottle on the hearth was pretty heavy-handed drama."

"Maybe so, but Larry was a dramatic person. It was his way of telling me he knew everything, and it scared me half to death. Then he said he wanted all of my inheritance, the money David and I live on. I couldn't . . ."

"This time you brought the hammer with you."

"No! It wasn't that way!"

"Yes, Paul, it was." I stepped forward, my gun extended. Collins stared. He blinked. His lips moved soundlessly.

"Let's go, Paul."

Desperately, he glanced from side to side. His eyes stopped at the lamp. He looked at me, back at it, and then he kicked out his foot. The lamp crashed to the floor. Flames shot up.

Collins launched his bulky body at me. He hit me face on, and my gun flew from my hand. We crashed into the wall. Above my head, a hammer smacked into the plaster.

The flames lapped at the boxes of books. I grabbed Collins' wrist. We wrestled for the hammer.

I grabbed its head and pulled hard. If the flames reached the half-full container of kerosene . . .

Collins tugged on the shaft. His hands began to slip.

With one last wrench, I pulled the hammer free. I careened across the room into the fireplace. Collins leapt for the door.

I dropped the hammer and scooped up my gun, jamming it into the waistband of my jeans. Stripping off my raincoat, I tossed it on the flames. I stamped at them with my feet and hands. By the time they were out, the front door had slammed.

I ran downstairs and outside. Mist and tangled vegetation obscured my vision. Then I saw Collins flailing down the walk.

"Stop!" I shouted, pulling out my gun. "Hold it, Paul!" I fired once into the air.

Collins turned, then altered course, running through a clump of pyracantha. I followed. He headed straight for the retaining wall.

"Paul, stop! You can't get away!"

He looked back, stumbled, grabbed for a branch. His hand missed, and I lost sight of him in the undergrowth. His footsteps staggered. I crashed through the bushes. Ahead of me, I heard a low cry that rose to a scream.

"Paul, hold it!"

A muffled thud followed.

I rushed back to the stairway and took it down two steps at a time. Even before I got to the crumpled body on the sidewalk, the odd angle of his neck told me Collins was dead.

26

I sat on the window seat in Greg's little redwood house on Twin Peaks, looking out at the city. It was very late, and from this distance San Francisco looked softly beautiful. The high-flying mist obscured what I knew was down there: the fleabag hotels, the winos on doorsteps, the rotting slums, the ugly sleeping secrets in places both high and humble.

I remembered Eleanor van Dyne's words about the spring Richard Wintringham had died: "It was a lovely spring; we'd never seen better. . . . The loveliness was such a contrast to what was happening there on Steiner Street. It made everything seem all the more terrible."

I shivered and raised my brandy glass, sipping deeply.

The postmidnight hours I had spent at the Hall of Justice, making my formal statement. One does not walk away from chasing a murder suspect over a cement wall to his death without first crawling through a maze of red tape, not even if the lieutenant on the case is a good friend. Greg had been matter of fact, throwing out none of his usual barbs, but still I'd had no easy time of it. His comments about me concealing evidence had been terse and stern. As I talked, I discovered I'd liked Paul Collins in spite of his murders. He was a gentle man, ill at ease with his nature, and ultimately the rough world had driven him too far. While knowing that did not excuse his crimes, it made them more understandable.

With that understanding came a cool, clear wave of sorrow that now washed over me again. I sipped brandy, stared at the city, and thought of David Wintringham.

When I'd emerged from Greg's office, I'd spotted David and Charmaine seated on a bench in the squad room. Wintringham leaned forward, his lanky arms dangling over his knees. Charmaine, still in the bloodstained jumpsuit, smoked and jiggled one crossed leg in a staccato rhythm. I went over to them.

"David," I said, "I'm sorry."

He looked up, his eyes dull as they had been after French's murder. "Don't be."

"But Paul . . ."

"No." He stood, taking both my hands in his. "I suspected Paul. Not consciously, but somewhere inside I've wondered ever since my father died. When Jake was killed, I verified Paul's alibi again, but I realized that both times he'd said he was in the house with me, and I'd merely seconded it, believing him. The first time, he claimed he'd been in the kitchen fixing tea. Even though we lived separately, we took our meals together, and he had brought me a cup that evening, although I wasn't really too clear on the time."

Wintringham paused. "Imagine, bringing a person a cup of tea after you've killed his father."

I shuddered. "What about the night Jake died? Where did he say he was?"

"Upstairs reading. I should have known. You can tell when there's another person in the house and when there's not. But I guess I didn't want to know." His hawk-like features twisted.

I held tight to his hands for a moment. "The Cheshire Cat's Eye," I finally said. "Was it badly damaged?"

"Not that much." Charmaine startled me by speaking. "I saw it when they brought it in here. It's fixable. Your raincoat is another story, however."

I remembered throwing it on the flames. "Doesn't matter."

Wintringham turned to Charmaine. "Do you think you could repair the lamp?"

"Sure." She stubbed out her cigarette and stood. "Send it around once the police release it." To me, she added, "They *will* give it back, won't they?"

"Eventually."

"Good." Wintringham dropped my hands and rubbed his together briskly. It was a gesture of getting on with his life. While it helped him now, I doubted he'd be able to return to normalcy so easily. About Charmaine I had no similar fears.

"You fix the lamp, Charmaine," Wintringham said. "Then I want Sharon to have it."

"But it's your family . . ." I began.

He shook his head. "It would be too painful for me to have it around. The Cheshire Cat should go to live at your house now."

Scarcely knowing what to say, I pictured the lamp as it had sat on my bureau: a gentle reminder of the old among the new. "Thank you, David." I turned toward the elevators, but someone touched my shoulder. I looked up at Greg.

"You all right?"

"Sure."

"Good." He placed a key in my hand and closed my fingers over it.

"What's that?"

"My house key. Why don't you go there and wait for me? Have a drink; you know where the liquor cabinet is."

"But I . . ."

"You don't want to be alone tonight."

Truthfully, I didn't. "Okay. I'll see you there."

"I won't be long."

When the elevator doors closed, Greg was still standing there, looking concerned and a little tired.

Now I heard the garage door open and, moments later, Greg's footsteps on the stairs. He crossed the room and flopped into an armchair next to me, rubbing his hand across his eyes.

"Is it all wrapped up?" I asked.

"Reasonably." He reached for my brandy glass and sipped. "We found the broken replica of the Tiffany lamp at French's apartment, stuffed behind some towels in a linen closet. Al Prince identified it as the one Jake Kaufmann borrowed from him. And we found bloodstained clothing between the mattress and the box spring in Collins' room. I've no doubt the blood will match the types of the last two victims, and that the hammer he threw at you will test out to be the murder weapon."

"And that, plus my statement and Wintringham's admission of his suspicions, will close all three files."

"Yeah." Greg handed the brandy back to me. "You had a lot of that?" He gestured at the glass.

I had, but it had left me strangely clearheaded. "Yes and no."

He nodded.

After a few minutes of silence, he said, "You'll never learn."

"Learn what?"

"Not to go running off chasing killers and putting yourself in danger."

"I tried to reach you when I figured out who it was, but you weren't taking calls."

"You could have waited."

"It's not in my nature to wait."

"I guess not." He stood up. "It's late, papoose. Let's go to bed."

I looked at his outstretched hand. There was something. . . . Oh, yes. "Are you sure the other cop would approve of that?" I asked acidly.

He stared. "Who?"

"Remember: Screwing a private eye is just like screwing another cop."

Greg began to laugh. "You are so goddamn literal-minded! That, papoose, was a figure of speech. I've never so much as touched another cop in my life."

"Oh? Well, then, what's that extra pillow and all the feminine gear doing . . . ?"

"I am delighted!"

"What?"

"I never thought you'd be jealous. This opens up whole new prospects—"

"I am not jealous!" I jumped up.

"Hush." He reached out an arm and pulled me close. "You're right; an explanation is in order. As you may recall, I've pursued you steadily these last months."

"Well, yes."

"And I didn't want to be caught unprepared."

"Boy Scout, huh?"

"So I went out, in anticipation of Saturday night, and bought a few necessities. If you'll look at the pillow, you'll find the 'under penalty of law' tag is still attached."

"Oh, for lord's sake."

"Of course, if you don't come to bed, you won't be able to verify that."

Blackmail. Subtle, but blackmail no less. I slipped my arm around Greg's waist as we started up the stairs.